CW00484798

Early Shift

Steve Higgs

Text Copyright © 2020 Steven J Higgs

Publisher: Steve Higgs

The right of Steve Higgs to be identified as author of the Work has been asserted by him in accordance with the Copyright, Designs and Patents Act 1988

All rights reserved.

The book is copyright material and must not be copied, reproduced, transferred, distributed, leased, licensed or publicly performed or used in any way except as specifically permitted in writing by the publishers, as allowed under the terms and conditions under which it was purchased or as strictly permitted by applicable copyright law. Any unauthorised distribution or use of this text may be a direct infringement of the author's and publisher's rights and those responsible may be liable in law accordingly.

'Early Shift' is a work of fiction. Names, characters, businesses, organisations, places, events and incidents either are the product of the author's imagination or are used fictitiously. Any resemblance to actual persons, living, dead or undead, events or locations is entirely coincidental.

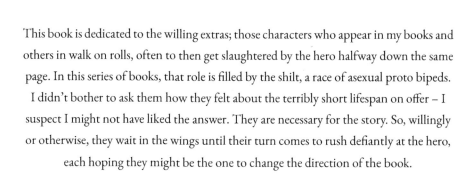

This book is dedicated to the willing extras; those characters who appear in my books and others in walk on rolls, often to then get slaughtered by the hero halfway down the same page. In this series of books, that role is filled by the shilt, a race of asexual proto bipeds. I didn't bother to ask them how they felt about the terribly short lifespan on offer – I suspect I might not have liked the answer. They are necessary for the story. So, willingly or otherwise, they wait in the wings until their turn comes to rush defiantly at the hero, each hoping they might be the one to change the direction of the book.

Contents

Chapter 1

March 2012, Hjepsted, Denmark

The sound of the trucks stopping woke him. He was in the barn where he slept every night. Mia and Moritz had long since given up trying to convince him to sleep in the house; he knew it was safer for them if he didn't.

Zachary didn't own a phone. He had no reason for one and hadn't bothered with a watch in years; time meant so little to him, but he didn't need either to know that it was the middle of the night; no time for people to be visiting unless they had an ill purpose.

The only question in his mind was whether they were here to run him off or intended to scare the old couple he worked for. It didn't really matter which it was, either way, Zachary was about to ruin their plan and then he would have to leave.

The moon lit the ground outside, peering through gaps between the slats of the barn, he could see them approaching. A dozen of them maybe; the men from the farming cooperative. Their appearance tonight came as no surprise; they were always going to show up at some point. Their boss wanted the old couple to move on. He needed their land for what he had planned and had been harassing them for some time. Zachary had stood up to them, slapped a few around when they pushed their luck, and now they were coming to even the score and get rid of the man who was preventing their success.

It wouldn't work out the way they wanted.

All he had on was a pair of underpants. He tossed them onto his pile of roughly folded clothes, huffed out a bored sigh, and went out to meet the men. A couple of them carried gasoline cans, planning to torch the barn with him in it perhaps.

As he stepped boldly into the moonlight, halting the advancing line of men, most feeling brave because there were so many of them, he could smell the alcohol on their breath. He scanned around slowly, counting the men, counting their weapons and making a note of who looked nervous and was likely to run and who looked determined and ready to fight. What he saw was a rabble. They had been in a bar before they came for him, their boss most likely going there to round them up. They were all big men, but more than half looked like they didn't want to be here, and the rest would find their reactions dulled by however much they had drunk this evening.

What they saw was a naked white man standing more than two metres tall. It showed off his muscularity, something Zachary came by naturally. He worked a lot of manual labour jobs, and that kept him lean, but he never went to the gym, not since he was in his early teens. When the change came to him at fourteen, there was little need for it, his muscles growing and swelling with no effort on his part. He kept his hair trim, the only self-grooming effort he ever expended, but wore his fringe long so it would sweep across to the left. It was a hairstyle he picked at fifteen and never changed.

One of the nearest men laughed. 'Well, there's something you don't see every night. Around here we wear clothes, boy.'

His companions laughed along with him, the line of men fanning out to partly surround him. Some of them looked like they could handle themselves, they might even have had some training. Not like his training, of course, and none of it would save them from what was almost certainly about to happen.

Zachary drew in a deep breath, letting it go slowly through his nose. The air was cold, it was March in Denmark after all, but he didn't feel the cold the same way others do; it didn't bother him at all.

He wanted to avoid the fight if he could, so he gave them a warning he knew they would ignore. 'You have one chance to get out of this unharmed. After that, remember you chose this path, not me.'

The men looked at each other for a second or so, glancing about in disbelief. There was a dozen of them and only one of him. They had weapons, and he didn't even have any clothes on.

Their leader - Potente, Zachary thought his name was, a big man with a big ego - laughed at him. 'I think you have this about-face, son. You can walk away. We won't hurt you, despite what you did to some of my boys.' Movement in the line revealed one of them was there tonight. The man bore an angry expression, his sneer unconvincing to Zachary's mind because of the black eyes and plaster across his nose. The other two got it worse and would still be in hospital. His attention was drawn back to Potente when he spoke, 'Go on now, get your things and leave.'

'Last chance, dickface,' Zachary replied. Then he closed his eyes and drew in a fresh breath. He could force the change when he concentrated, accelerating the time it took to shift between forms to produce an effect that was terrifying for those who saw it. He waited until Potente started to speak again and then he did it.

Surrounded by men who thought themselves hard, he funnelled the magic inside his body, causing it to transform. Shocked gasps of surprise reached his ears, but then it was done. It hurt doing it so fast, but he was used to pain.

Standing where the naked man had been was a two and a half metre tall werewolf. Golden light glowed like veins beneath his now black skin, shining out from beneath the coarse hair that covered his body. His eyes glowed deep red, like pits of burning embers but his hands drew the most attention. Each finger ended in a fifteen-centimetre claw that resembled a dagger. They were black like onyx and the moonlight glinted off them as he raised his arms and leapt.

In a conventional fight, like he'd with the three men at the bar just two days ago, he would assess who would get to him first or presented the greatest threat. Not that any of them could easily hurt him. He was quite literally impossible to kill, but he wasn't impervious to injury. In his human form, he could be cut or stabbed or shot. An incident with a demon a couple of months ago had changed him, making him somehow immortal, at least that was what he had come to believe. He used to heal quickly, but a stab wound would still take days to repair. Now, he healed almost as soon as the blade left the wound. Within minutes, certainly. In werewolf form, he was tougher still, but more than that; he was fast. Really fast and that meant that most men couldn't hurt him no matter what they did.

A dozen men came to deal with him. Beating them would be easy. The hard bit would be not killing anyone.

As his leap carried him through the air, some of the men simply turned and fled, terror gripping their feet to make them run. However, Potente stood his ground, his reputation as top dog to uphold, and he wasn't the only one. Annoyingly, a gun appeared in Potente's hand as Zachary came back to earth. He wasn't the only one carrying a firearm and as Zachary landed, the silent night sky suddenly filled with thunderous gunfire as the man to Potente's left took aim and fired.

Panic or lack of discipline on the man's part meant he missed. Three rounds fired rapidly in panic and with little control. Potente also pulled his trigger but his aim was no better. They would get him soon enough if he stayed still, but he wasn't going to do that.

Zachary ducked as another shot was fired, then jinked left, and slashed at the man next to Potente with his left arm. His claws raked across the man's chest and down to his abdomen, leaving a wound he felt certain would put him in the hospital for a week. He was a blur of movement, continuing his spin, pivoting off one foot until he was back facing Potente. His right arm was travelling at the furthest point of the circle he prescribed, whipping around too fast for Potente to see or hope to avoid. Zachary straightened himself and stabbed his right hand directly into Potente. The move violated his desire to leave the man alive, but where he could so easily have killed him with the first blow, he aimed for the leader's shoulder instead, skewering him with four claws where the arm meets the chest. Potente's scream filled the air as he dropped his gun, no longer able to hold it.

He could so easily rip the man in two at this point; he didn't deserve the leniency Zachary was showing him, but then Zachary wasn't doing it for Potente. He was doing it for himself. Despite everything, he wasn't a killer. Not if he could help it.

Only two of the men stayed to fight the enormous creature, a demonstration that they were braver than they were bright. As they fell to the ground, crying in pain and bleeding into the soil, Zachary assumed it was over, but at the trucks, some of the men running for their lives had assumed firing positions.

Too late to stop them, Zachary realised a barrage of shots was about to come his way just half a second before it happened. Cursing his arrogance, he had no choice but to charge them; he was in open ground and an easy target. Each bullet strike hurt, he felt one glance off his left femur as it went through his leg and it caused him to stumble a pace, but most of the shots still missed him and he needed only another second to close the distance to the nearest man.

The man's eyes filled with terror as he held his trigger on, missed with all but one shot as the werewolf lunged for him, and heard his weapon click to empty. The roar of engines reached his ears as his companions abandoned him, peeling away from the nightmare as fast as they could make their pickup trucks and vans go.

When the magazine emptied, Zachary had been about to slash the man with the claws of his giant right hand, but seeing his colleagues flee, and the look of stark horror on the face of the man facing him, he stopped himself. He would remember it as one of the hardest things he'd done in a long time. These hard men deserved to be hurt, picking on an old couple because their farmland was inconveniently placed for someone else's plans.

Zachary looked down at the frightened face and asked, 'What do you think will happen if I ever see you again?'

The man just gulped, too terrified to form words.

Behind him, Potente and the other injured man were still groaning but Zachary didn't think their wounds were life-threatening provided they got medical help soon. 'Get them and go,' he growled. Then added. 'Now!' when the man failed to move, aiming a kick at his butt as he ran to collect Potente.

The fight was over. Dozens of shots had been fired, and lights were on in the house across the yard where Mia and Moritz were undoubtedly throwing clothes on and fishing out their old shotgun.

There was one last thing to do, then it would be time for him to assess his wounds, pack his things and leave. As the leader, Potente, came back toward the waiting pickup supported under his good shoulder by the man Zachary had allowed to live, he stopped him. 'I warned you,' Zachary hissed into Potente's face. 'Why didn't you listen?' Potente didn't have a reply, he was trying his best to look mean and defiant, but Zachary felt sure he would never return.

They all heard the farmhouse door open, Moritz firing his shotgun into the air as a show of aggression even before he saw the scene outside.

Zachary turned their way which was enough to stop them both in the imagined safety of their doorway. He sighed, disappointed that he would have to move on yet again.

Turning his back on Potente, Zachary said, 'Don't come back,' and trudged to the barn to get his things. Potente wouldn't be back but that didn't mean the old couple were free of future troubles. There was nothing he could do to protect them from a large, money-backed cooperative who wanted to force them off their land. Not without killing a stack of people and that wasn't his purpose in life.

Two minutes later, he emerged from the barn in human form, his clothes on and his few possessions packed into a backpack slung over one shoulder.

The men and the trucks were gone, a few dark stains on the frozen ground the only sign that the fight had ever taken place. Mia and Moritz were inside their house, peering carefully out of a window at the barn where moments ago they saw a monster go.

They couldn't hide the surprise on their faces when they saw Zachary coming out of it now. His secret was out; there was no way to take it back. He didn't think the old couple would talk about it much, not even to each other, but they knew, and they would never feel safe with him around again. Even if they had been able to get their heads around it, staying now would only bring more trouble their way. Law enforcement would be here in a few hours, the best thing he could do for them was leave.

Either way, Zachary was moving on, leaving the country.

He knocked lightly on the farmhouse door, calling out to the old couple inside, 'Mia, Moritz, it's Zachary. I just wanted to let you know I am leaving. You should head back to bed; the danger is over. But you need to report that Potente and his men were here.' He wanted to say more, he wanted to wish them luck, but he knew the best thing he could do was just start walking.

Less than two metres from their door, he heard it open. The cautious sound of someone opening it just a crack so they could peer out. He turned to find Moritz framed in the light from the room behind him. Mia was peering around his shoulder.

Moritz still clutched the shotgun in his hands, but he said, 'I owe you money, young man.'

It was true, he did. Zachary didn't have much use for the money since they fed him all his meals as part of the deal, so there were unclaimed wages which might be useful now he was leaving. Despite that, Zachary said, 'That's okay.'

Moritz frowned at him. 'This ain't no charity, son. You worked harder than any man we ever had on the farm. I ought to be paying you triple, the amount of work you did in a day. Just hold on a moment while I fetch it.'

He waited, he took the money, and he shook the old man's hand. There was the inevitable suggestion that he wait until morning, or could Moritz give him a lift somewhere, but Zachary was used to his lifestyle, so he thanked him once again, said goodbye, and started walking.

Tomorrow he would be somewhere else, Germany perhaps. That wasn't far to go from here and being in a different country would dilute any heat that might be following. As he started walking, he remembered a tabloid news article he read online about a wolf sighting. That had been somewhere in North Germany. Maybe he could check that out.

Chapter 2

Each night they waited for her to come. Sometimes she did and other times they were disappointed.

'Do you think she'll show?' asked Peter, keeping his head down and his eyes on the ground as she liked it.

His eldest brother huffed out a breath of annoyance. 'If I didn't, why on earth would I be kneeling here waiting for her, you idiot?' Horst found his youngest brother tiresome. Growing up, the boys had all been treated harshly by their father, a man who was quick to use the rod whenever he felt inclined. It made the four boys into hardened men. By the time they reached their late teens they were men who were capable and strong and unchallenged by anyone with a jot of sense. Then, ten years after his youngest brother's birth, came the unexpected one. Peter didn't get the rod; his father had grown old and soft by then, so Horst took it upon himself to make sure the newest addition to his clan grew up tough and strong. He failed though, his youngest brother somehow lacking the muscle and fibre that the rest of them possessed in spades.

'How long do we wait?' whispered Peter, making Horst want to punch him.

It was Hans that answered, 'Until we can be certain she isn't coming.'

Silence returned and they waited.

Horst was getting impatient and doing his best not to show that his knees were starting to hurt. Counting off in his head, he was going to give it another minute, and that was when it happened.

The sound of air rippling was followed by the sound of feet on the dirt ahead of him.

A woman's voice said, 'You may rise.'

Obediently, all five brothers raised their heads. Ahead of them was a beautiful woman in her early forties and behind her was a shimmering circle of air she had just emerged from. It looked like water on a lake hung vertically. As they watched silently, her left hand moved and the portal closed with a barely audible pop, the circle shrinking in on itself to reveal the far wall of their barn behind it.

'Show me,' she demanded.

All five men got to their feet. Horst nodding to Peter to go first.

The youngest brother looked nervous as he lifted his hands, casting his eyes about to his brothers and wishing he didn't have to go at all because he knew he was going to fail.

Watching him, the woman said, 'Conjure air.'

'Air,' Peter repeated nervously to himself as he concentrated, trying to remember what she had taught him. He could feel the energy deep in the earth. She said he ought to be able to see it, but he couldn't, he didn't know how to bring up the second sight she described. Five sets of eyes were watching him, judging him as he tried to use the energy he could feel to produce air.

'Don't force it,' she instructed, a touch of impatience already in her voice. 'Let the ley line flow through you. Form it in your mind and reach out with your senses to touch it.'

Peter began to sweat from the effort, desperately trying to work out how to do what everyone wanted him to do. He stole a glance at Rolf, the middle of the five brothers and the only one that ever came to his defence. Even *his* face looked disappointed.

'Enough,' the woman snapped.

Peter dropped his arms, 'I'm sorry, Rebecca. I...'

She murmured a word, 'Incensus,' and he collapsed where he stood, all ability to control his body taken from him. 'You will address me as mistress.'

He couldn't respond, couldn't apologise, even his mouth didn't work. Only his organs and his eyes were operational as he lay on the cold dirt floor of the barn unable even to blow away the piece of straw now irritating his nose.

Rebecca turned her attention to Rolf. 'Now you.' Her voice was sweet now, flirtatious even as she coaxed the best from the remaining four brothers. Each of them took their turn to produce an air spell before she moved on to water.

All Peter could do was watch, forgotten and ignored in the dirt as she praised them for their advancing abilities. She kept him like that for more than an hour as she trained the others, helping them to focus and improve. When she was done and it was time for them to taste her, she whispered the word to release him, 'Incantus.' All his muscles came back to life instantly, feeling flooding back.

He knew what he had to do. Quickly rolling onto his knees, he bowed his head and thanked her. 'Thank you, mistress.'

There was no response from her or from his brothers as they too got on their knees to form a semi-circle in front of her. Stopping in front of Horst, she performed her own magic, pulling what she referred to as Earth's source energy through her body. It crackled and arced across her skin, showing through her clothes as it came down her arms. As she did every time, she produced a blade in her left hand, a black object, curved almost like a sickle. It dug into the flesh of her right palm, opening the skin and Horst reached up to hold her fingers as her blood dripped from them into his mouth.

Each brother got the same, even Peter, who didn't want to but couldn't ever express his desire to avoid what they were becoming. Rebecca said they were special, that with training they could become powerful and would be able to rule and Horst believed they were going to be gods.

Months ago, when she first came to them, she made them all agree to be her students, pricking their thumbs and holding them to her chest where she now had five red marks, like brands or tattoos; their thumbprints indelibly etched onto her skin. The brothers celebrated her and worshipped her, all except Peter, who wondered just what was in store for them and what it was that she got from this deal.

He couldn't say that though. He couldn't raise a single question. Not without getting a beating from Horst.

Horst and his brothers ran their village. Everyone in it knew to be polite and courteous and to make sure they did as they were told. They owned almost everything, either wholly or in part. Over many years, they had found ways to make the locals bend to their will, offering incentives when necessary, threatening often and always, always, scheming to be unchallenged. The last man to stand up to them went missing the very same night. The story the villagers got was that he chose to leave, but Peter knew that wasn't true. He saw what they did to him – what he did to him, for in failing to stop them, he took part too.

As Peter wandered back to the farmhouse and his bed, his brothers still in the barn revelling in how well they had all done tonight, he worried for what Horst might do with his newfound abilities and what it might mean for the local community. His four older brothers already employed ninety percent of the villagers in one way or another. There was only one business left they hadn't been able to crack but they had a plan for that too. Add magic to their ruthlessness and who could possibly challenge them?

Lying awake, Peter had no idea that the answer to that question would soon wander into the village looking for work.

Chapter 3

Z achary spent most of his time avoiding people when he could. It was a personal choice thing. He was dangerous, he knew that. He had been since his age hit double figures and he had a short fuse. His past was littered with fights and arrests and brief stints in jail. Even now he knew there was an outstanding warrant for his arrest in Bulgaria.

He wasn't in Bulgaria though and he never planned to go back. Too many bad memories waited there for him. For almost a decade, since his teens, in fact, he had been moving about, never staying anywhere too long because there was always some kind of trouble as if it followed him around.

Leaving Hjepsted in the early hours of this morning he caught a lift with a lorry driver on the A419 road leading away from the coast. He didn't expect his thumb to attract much attention, not at that time of night, but the eighteen-wheeler, driven by a big man with an even bigger beard, pulled to a stop just a hundred metres ahead. Zachary jogged to get to the cab, the German number plate giving him hope that he might get lucky first time.

His plan had been to walk all the way to the motorway. There was one, the number eleven he thought, which ran directly north to south through Denmark and would carry him over the border and into Germany. There would be a service station somewhere along the road and there he would find a truck driver willing to have company for a few hours. Serendipity interrupted that plan and saved him at least two hours of walking.

'Where're you heading?' asked a mouth hidden somewhere inside the impressive beard.

'Doesn't really matter,' Zachary replied, his voice a rumbling bass. 'Germany would be good, but beyond that, I just need somewhere quiet and out of the way where I can find some casual labour. I'm on a gap year,' he lied, hoping that would explain things. 'I'm getting out and seeing Europe while I'm still young.'

Zachary wasn't sure the man believed him; he looked a little old for a student at twenty-seven, but he accepted it and let him in. 'It'll be about three hours to the border. I can let you out anywhere after that. You just tell me when you like the look of someplace.'

'Where're you heading?' Zachary asked in return.

The driver pointed out of his windshield, indicating the road ahead. Zachary thought that he was going to leave it at that, but the beard cracked open again to say, 'Hannover. I get a bonus if get there before lunch, so I don't even need to rush.'

Zachary didn't know how far it was to Hannover, his mental map telling him it was to the north of Germany but not all the way north. It was warm in the cab, and quiet, the driver happy to eat up the kilometres without conversation.

Presently, Zachary slept.

When he opened his eyes again it was light out. A horn blast had woken him and as his eyes focused, he could see traffic stretching into the distance, none of it moving.

'It's roadworks,' announced the driver. 'That and probably some fool crashed into someone else so now we have a double problem. This might take a while to get through.'

Sitting up and twisting his neck to get the cricks out, Zachary squinted into the distance where he could see a road sign. It was too far away to read though, even with his superior eyesight. 'Where are we?'

'Just past Soltau.'

Zachary shook his head. 'I don't know where that is.'

The beard split into a grin and the driver lifted a meaty right hand to lift his ballcap and scratch his balding head. 'About halfway between Hamburg and Hannover. Do you know where they are?'

Zachary had worked a job in Hamburg a few years back, once again his size getting him hired to hump and dump on the quayside without the need for an interview. When he didn't answer, the driver frowned and glanced across at his large passenger. 'You running from something? Some kind of trouble?'

Obviously, he hadn't bought the gap year story or had been thinking about it ever since. Looking out the window at a friendly looking Labrador in the boot of a BMW, Zachary said, 'Trouble tends to find me. Even when I hide.'

All the driver did was nod.

The traffic crept forward, the road sign coming closer until Zachary could read it. 'What's in Bad Dorstel?' It was the next exit, coming up in two kilometres and the name sounded familiar for some reason. Suddenly the memory came back to him. Bad Dorstel was the name of the place where he read about a werewolf being seen. In his entire life he had only ever met one other werewolf; a person with the ability to shift their form. That was just two months ago in Bremen and it ended badly. Until he heard about it and went running to Bremen, he had all but given up bothering to search.

The ability to shift came to him just before his fourteenth birthday. Anger caused it the first time when he faced down three older boys he didn't know as they surrounded a boy from his class. It was childish nonsense; they probably didn't intend the boy any real harm, they were just being boys, bullying smaller kids because it made them feel big, but he hated that sort of thing. He always had. In fact, he couldn't remember a time when he hadn't singled out the bullies and faced them down and he didn't care how big they were in comparison either. Once, he took on a man in the street when he was out playing on his bicycle. He couldn't have been more than six or maybe seven years old but heard the man shouting at his wife or girlfriend and rode over to intervene.

The man slapped his face when Zachary told him to back away, gripping the woman's arm even as she cried and begged him to let go because he was hurting her. The slap had stung but when he ran at the man and kicked his shin, then continued to pummel his groin and gut because they were at the right height for him, the man let go of the woman. He tried to swat Zachary but whatever he did made no difference to the enraged child and the man ran off. The event imbued Zachary with a feeling of righteousness he had never shifted and though he didn't know where his sense of right and wrong came from, he felt certain he was right.

So, aged fourteen, when the three bullies picked on the boy in his class, Zachary stormed in, shoving the boy in the middle so he fell backwards to the ground and then he growled at the remaining two. That was when it happened. He intended to show them his teeth, growling into their faces to give them a chance to run away rather than hand out a beating and wind up being taken home by the police for the umpteenth time. The growl came out different to normal though, it sounded guttural, like a large dog had made it, and the boys' reaction was to scream in terror, running away so fast they stumbled and fell.

It startled him that first time, but he felt the change, felt his face rearrange itself and when he glanced at his hands, they weren't his hands anymore; they were like his but bigger, the fingers longer and his nails had grown to form talons.

He hid them quickly; glad he had a hoody to hide his face from the classmate still standing behind him.

'Are you okay, Zachary?' the boy had asked.

Zachary didn't know how to answer and wasn't sure what his voice would do if he tried to speak, but as he tried to quell his rising panic, he could feel that his face and hands were returning to normal.

'I'm fine,' he replied, turning around to face the smaller boy. Then he excused himself and ran home. After that, he learned to bring on the change at will, but also found it very hard to control when he got angry. The monster beneath the surface of his skin wanted to be set free whenever Zachary was challenged.

He used the internet to search for other shifters, imagining that there must be more than just him out there, but after months of finding wannabe sex-fantasy forums and Live

Action Role Play groups, he gave up. Even searching through newspaper articles and reading daft paranormal conspiracy publications gave him no sense that he wasn't the only one on the planet.

All he had for reference was old movies, Bela Lugosi or Oliver Reed playing the wolfman to name just two. It was all nonsense though, none of the facts correct. He didn't need the moonlight to change, and he didn't have to change under a full moon. One idea stuck with him though: the idea for the werewolf hadn't been dreamed up, it had been based on reality. Research into the origin of the legend went back thousands of years to Greek mythology. Had there been werewolves then and that early legend was based on a true story?

Zachary didn't expect to ever know the answer, but he looked into every report he could find until he left home aged seventeen and then went to some of the places he thought might yield a result. He wanted to find someone like him – he couldn't be the only one.

But he was. That was the conclusion he drew as search after search turned up no result. In the end, he just stopped looking. Then, two months ago, there were reports of murders in Bremen, a city he had just left, and it bore all the hallmarks of a werewolf attack. The paranormal websites he hadn't looked at for years were all over it, conspiracy theories abounding.

He went there, he found her, and finally he knew he wasn't alone. He lost her though and now he was alone again, but it gave him renewed vigour to find another. That was what took him to Hjepsted, a rumour of a bipedal beast, but it proved to be another tall tale. Bad Dorstel would most likely be the same, but he was here now.

The driver considered Zachary's question. 'Bad Dorstel? Not much. It's a potato growing region. There used to be a big Army barracks there, a British one. It's long gone now, of course, but I think the town collapsed once the soldiers left, all the bars and shops closed. There's nothing left now but the small farming community surrounding a tiny village.'

It sounded perfect. 'Can you let me out there?'

'Sure,' the driver laughed. 'You might as well get out and walk though at the pace we are going.'

Zachary laughed too, a small outrush of breath with a smile. He thanked the driver, shook his hand and climbed out just as the traffic started to move. Whatever had been blocking the road had been moved, so the moment his feet hit the tarmac, the truck lurched forward and picked up speed as the driver changed gear.

Smiling at the irony, Zachary jogged to the hard shoulder and started walking.

He needed breakfast. That was the first thing to deal with. Mia and Moritz had fed him every meal for weeks, so he had no snacks of his own. He did have money in his pocket and the expectation that he would find somewhere selling food.

He should have stayed on the truck.

Chapter 4

'Morning,' the woman pouring the coffee said as he came through the door.

Walking into the village, if one could call it that, took more than an hour, his hunger growing with every step. The route took him past the old garrison fence line, the buildings behind it looking abandoned and overgrown.

His nose led him onwards, the keen sense of smell another attribute that went with his supernatural nature. Bacon - that was what he could smell, though he couldn't yet tell if it was someone's kitchen or an eatery until he came out from the fence line he followed, through some trees and found himself facing a diner-looking building. It had wide windows all along the front façade, through which he could see people sitting at tables. Many of them were eating, and as he watched, a young woman came into sight with a coffee pot, topping off mugs as she went.

He had seen places like this before in other farming communities. Lots of transient workers without the means to easily cook for themselves meant opportunity for profit. They always served simple meals, peasant food really, but it was generally wholesome, stick-to-your-ribs fare the workers needed for the manual labour they were about to perform.

Hunger driving him onwards, he was going in to get breakfast even if, ultimately, he decided that he wasn't going to stay.

Zachary made his way across the room to the single diner counter at the front. Every set of eyes turned to watch him cross the room. It was his size that drew the attention. Everywhere he went, people stared. At over two metres, he was by far the tallest man in any room, but he was so broad across his shoulders and chest that he looked like two men glued together. He gave up trying to blend in years ago, accepting that his freakish size, combined with his supernatural nature, meant he needed to live on the fringes of society, keeping his contact with people to a minimum.

'Passing through or stopping for a while?' asked a voice as Zachary put his bag down and manoeuvred onto a stool. It was the young woman who'd been serving coffee. She'd placed the pot back onto the warming plate and was bustling behind the counter now.

'Yes. I'm looking for some farm work if you know of any.' He figured this would be the best place to find work if there was any. In a place this size, where he was currently sitting had to be the hub for all activity. Half the population would pass through here most days.

Two stools along, a man leaned forward, sizing Zachary up, his eyes narrowed, and he quickly reached a conclusion. 'I can offer you work,' he said. Zachary was looking at the woman when the man said it, so got to see the flicker of worry in her eyes. She looked away quickly, hurrying off to collect an order as the chef behind the hatch called for service. 'Got any special skills?' asked the man.

Zachary turned on his stool to look at the man addressing him. The man was in his mid-forties and bigger than medium build, but not by much. On his stool, it was difficult to access his height, but it couldn't be any more than a metre eighty. He had the look of someone who was used to being outdoors, which made sense in this rural setting where Zachary expected most people worked on farms, but he also looked a little flabby and soft which suggested he was a boss and not someone doing any of the manual labour himself. His hair was receding and what remained was pulled into a ponytail. It was not a look that did the man any favours in Zachary's opinion, but it didn't require comment. To answer the man, he said, 'I'm good with animals. I can drive a tractor. I'm strong.'

The man put out his hand. 'Hans Koch.'

'Zachary Barnabus.'

Hans Koch looked Zachary up and down before settling on his eyes. 'Where's that accent from? You're not local.'

Zachary didn't like answering questions about himself, but he would let one or two slip now while he worked out if there was work here or not. 'Hungary originally.'

Hans seemed satisfied by the answer, sitting back down on his stool again. 'I dare say you are strong. There're no animals here though. There's not a lot of farm work at all, truth be told. It's off season around here. I have ... other work that a man your size might be interested in, depending on your skills and morals.'

The subtext was barely hidden in the man's words, Zachary picked up on it instantly because he was supposed to; the man was suggesting intimidation work of some kind. Or maybe even enforcement work where he would be expected to break bones. He shook his head. 'No, thank you. I just want something quiet and out of the way.'

'I have an opening here doing bar work, if you are interested,' said the woman behind the counter.

Zachary was happy to take his attention away from the man. It wouldn't be the first time he had worked in a bar, but he tended to shy away from work that put him into contact with drunken men. Sooner or later a fight would break out and that always bought out his aggressive side. Especially if he saw a man being aggressive toward a woman. He wasn't sure where the instinctual need to protect women came from, but it was there. Maybe it was something to do with the wolf, but whatever the case he learned long ago to avoid bars.

He wanted to politely decline so he could look for something that might suit him better, but Hans interrupted before he could. 'No, Gitta. You can't employ that brute here.' He said it like he was the owner or manager and it was his decision to make. He also growled the instruction which Zachary didn't like.

Gitta's eyes flashed with anger as she whipped her head across to snarl, 'You don't own this bar yet, Hans.'

Instantly angry, Hans shoved back his stool and stood up, jutting his face across the counter. 'That's just a matter of days, Gitta. Don't go making things worse for yourself now.'

Zachary had given it a two count, just to see if the man would calm down, but his grace period expired, so before Gitta could respond to Hans's latest threat, Zachary also pushed back his stool and stood up. Of course, when Zachary did it, he kept on standing up until he had reached his two metre ten height and looked down on everyone.

Hans's eyes swung across and then up to look at Zachary. Once he had the smaller man's attention, Zachary said, 'You are being impolite.' He didn't growl, he didn't need to. He uttered the words calmly, showing that he was in complete control.

Hans, unlike anyone else Zachary had ever spoken down to, wasn't cowed by his size which surprised the shifter. There was a man between them, but unbidden, he elected to get up, carrying his half-eaten breakfast and half-drunk cup of coffee, to another table. It struck Zachary as odd but the man now looking at him with an uninterrupted view was creating a void; all around them, people were trying to be somewhere else, some deciding they didn't want their breakfast after all as they elected to just leave.

Gitta saw her diner emptying and huffed with annoyance.

Zachary took it all in as he watched Hans. Then the smaller man did something Zachary didn't expect. He stepped forward to poke him in the chest. 'You'll find nothing here but trouble. Go back to where you came from or go somewhere else. If I see you in here again...'

'Yes?' asked Zachary, keen for the man to finish his threat. He could feel the heat inside his body, begging him to allow the change to start.

'Stop!' yelled Gitta. 'No fighting in here.'

As Hans turned his head to look at her, Zachary whipped his right arm up to engulf the hand prodding his chest. He didn't turn it or twist it, he just squeezed. Hans tried to resist reacting, but as the bones in his hand began to mash into each other, he started to slap at Zachary's arm. For Zachary, it was like being attacked by an angry fly.

'That's enough,' insisted Gitta, raising her voice to get the message across.

Zachary let him go, Hans instantly backing up a pace as he rubbed his hand and scowled. Then he snatched his wallet and keys off the counter and started toward the door. 'Don't employ him here, Gitta. There'll be trouble if you do.'

The door slammed hard behind him and Zachary sat on his stool once more. 'I'll take one of those tasty-looking breakfast plates, please.'

Gitta stared at him open mouthed. 'Really? You just scared off ninety percent of my clients. Now you want some breakfast?'

'Yes, please. I'll take that job too. You say it is bar work mostly?'

She looked exasperated, but Zachary was looking at her properly for the first time and couldn't help but notice how attractive he found her. Her skin had a radiant quality that only a person in their youth can achieve. He figured she was in her early twenties somewhere but whatever her age, he wasn't blind to her tight waist, long legs and shapely chest. At roughly a meter eighty tall, she was on the tall side for a woman and he liked that. Her chestnut brown hair was lustrous and shone with the low winter sun coming through the windows. It matched her deep brown eyes and she had a slender neck that he wanted to run his lips over.

He filed all that away quickly and made sure he was looking at her face.

'You worked in a bar before?' she asked, flinging a small towel over her shoulder as she moved to a hatch in the wall behind her. She bent down to call through it, 'Hey, mum. Another breakfast plate.'

A voice echoed back out. 'Has he gone?'

'You mean Hans? Yes, he left.'

'Is there going to be trouble?' her mum asked.

Gitta looked at Zachary, assessing him critically, pursing her lips and moving them from side to side before reaching an answer, 'Yes, probably.'

'Dammit.'

Zachary couldn't see her mother but caught a glimpse of a hand as his plate came through the hatch. He was curious about the dynamics at play and wanted to ask questions. Hunger ruled though, so as the platter of potato, eggs, veggies, and bacon landed in front of him, the questions went on hold.

Eating gave him time to think. His golden rule was to avoid trouble. Avoid fights. It wasn't impossible to fight without transforming, but the beast inside tried to get out every time he felt threatened. If it was over quickly, he was generally okay, and most fights were over quickly, but it was still a better policy to avoid the fight altogether. The probability of ending up in a fight here seemed high, Hans didn't seem the sort to let an insult lie. But there was something going on with the bar and the attractive woman and maybe her mother. So, he was going to stick around for a short while and see what was what. Besides, maybe there *was* a shifter here. It wouldn't take him more than a few days to figure that out for himself. He could do a little work, earn a little cash, maybe get to know Gitta a little and if he had to deal with Hans Koch, then he would move on afterward instead of moving on now.

Gitta left him alone to enjoy his meal, moving around the diner to collect half-finished breakfasts and chat with those customers who chose to remain, apologising unnecessarily, Zachary thought, to each of them for the less than peaceful start to their day.

When she came back to collect his empty plate, he said, 'That was good. Can I have another, please?'

Her eyebrows raised and she wanted to question how hungry he was. Then she considered that he was twice the size of the average person and the average person would finish one plate. She communicated his order through the hatch and came back to lean on the counter in front of him. 'Did I hear your name is Zachary?'

'Yes. And you're Gitta,' he replied. 'Is there something I should know about Mr Ponytail?'

Gitta placed a coffee cup in front of him and filled it from a jug. 'Yes. He has four brothers.'

Chapter 5

Zachary ate his second breakfast in quiet, let it sit for a while, and decided two plates was enough. The diner slowly emptied; the breakfast rush already past its peak by the time he arrived. Two heaping plates and three coffees later, he was finally sated and there was only one person left in the diner, an old man reading a newspaper way off in the corner.

He continued to wait. Gitta fetched empty plates to go back through the hatch where a pair of hands was now taking them back. It was the same pair of hands Zachary had seen providing the plates of food earlier.

Another half hour passed and, finally, Gitta ran out of things to do and stopped, blowing an errant hair from her face as she leaned back against the counter opposite him. She was eyeing him critically, which was fine because he had been doing the same to her. To her mind, he looked brutish, too big and too blocky to be attractive, but he was certainly a man who a woman could feel safe with. Provided the man wasn't the type who would hurt a woman.

'What's your story?' she asked, making it sound like she didn't really care and was asking to be polite.

He flipped his eyebrows, letting a smile play across his lips when he replied. 'I'm a werewolf on the run from trouble I caused in Denmark last night. This seems like a nice quiet place to hide out for a while.'

She raised one eyebrow. 'Fine. Keep secrets. You got a place to stay?'

'Not yet.'

'There's rooms here. Two of them, you can take your pick. The last guy left some stuff in one so you might want to take the other, but it's the smaller one.' She looked him up and down again. 'You look like you need all the room you can get.' She was already making her way across the room to a door in the back wall close to the bar. 'Come on, I'll show you.'

As she led him through to the back of the building, away from the public part, a little girl appeared.

'Mommy!' she cried, running to wrap her arms around Gitta's legs. The little girl had tousled, chestnut brown locks just like her mother and the same button nose. There was no mistaking who her mother was; Zachary could have picked her out of a crowd. He didn't have much experience with children but had never shied away from them either. She looked to be about three years old, but rather than guess, he asked.

Crouching, so his right knee was on the floorboards, he was still much taller than the little girl, but she looked up at him with friendly, if curious, eyes. 'Hello. I'm Zachary and I'm twenty-seven.'

The little girl just stared at him.

Gitta prodded her gently, smiling because her daughter's antics amused her constantly. 'Hey there. Hello. Earth to Paula. You are supposed to say something when people talk to you.'

She looked up at her mother. 'He looks funny. Why is he so big?'

Zachary sniggered. 'I am quite big,' he acknowledged. 'It's because I always eat all my vegetables.'

Paula gasped, her head and eyes swinging back to stare at his, 'That's what my mommy always says.' She uttered the words like it was an earth-shattering revelation. Then, the moment past, she turned and skipped away, her attention span already distracted by something else.

As Zachary stood up again, Gitta said, 'That's my little girl, Paula. She's three. You'll have to forgive her.'

'Nothing to forgive her for, she's adorable.'

His comment caught Gitta by surprise. Having a child at nineteen hadn't been her plan and for the most part it put men off; they seemed to see her as something used or worn now. She pushed the thought from her mind. 'The rooms are just up here.'

Going up the stairs, she explained about operating hours and basic duties. She was the manager for the diner and worked a split shift. They didn't open at all between ten in the morning and six in the evening and would get a rush of people at both points. The bar work itself was minimal, they didn't get too much evening business, except on a Friday. It was Friday today, so he should expect to be busy tonight. She would be there too, so he wouldn't be left to fend for himself. Apart from that, he was required to help out around the place.

She had him move some beer kegs around, doing her best not to comment when he picked up two in each hand and carried them like they were empty. He brought in supplies when her mum came back from a run to the nearest town, but then there nothing else for him to do. She was heading to her room to study, she said.

'What's the deal with Hans?' he asked as she took off her apron. They were standing in a lobby/hallway behind the scenes and somewhere close to the kitchen. His werewolf nose could pick up all the smells from it, bacon fat, cleaning fluid, onions.

She paused in her movement. To Zachary it looked like she had flinched. Then she started moving again, folding her apron, thinking better of it and screwing it up to go into the laundry. 'What are you asking?' she said as she fluffed her hair out of the back of her coat's collar.

It was a direct question. One of those, let's-not-beat-around-the-bush type of questions that killed off all need for pretence.

'I saw him make a grab for you earlier and his presence in the room made everyone else wary. Is he dangerous? Aggressive?'

'Yes,' she shrugged. 'Both of those probably and more. His brothers own or part own everything here. Everyone works for them in some way and they are tough, nasty sons of bitches you don't want to get on the wrong side of.' She looked him up and down again. 'You already did that though, didn't you? Hans will be back at some point and he will bring his brothers. They might start something, or they might just threaten you. Hans is one of the nicer ones. It's Horst you have to look out for. He's the eldest and the meanest. He likes to think he is mayor of the town or the patriarch. The last barman had a disagreement with him one night a week ago. The next day he left town. Or, at least, the Koch brothers told us he left town, but his things are still upstairs so they either ran him out of town too terrified to come by and grab his possessions or...'

'Or?'

'Or you can fill in the blanks for yourself. There's no law here. We are ten kilometres from the nearest police station, and no one here would call them if they thought the Kochs might find out who made the call. I need some sleep and I have books to read. If you're still here in six hours, I'll show you around the bar.'

His voice stopped her before she could escape. 'You said his family own everything here. They don't own this bar though?'

'No,' she replied, sounding very certain about it.

He hadn't imagined what he heard earlier and wanted to know more. Even if she thought it wasn't really his business, it was the reason he had stayed. 'Hans said it was a matter of days,' he prompted.

Gitta narrowed her eyes at him. Who was he to be asking such direct questions five minutes after walking into the place? 'You don't need to know about that.'

'You might as well just tell him, Gitta,' said her mother, coming into the hallway from packing away the supplies in the kitchen. 'Everyone in the village knows. He'll find out when he asks the first person to walk in tonight.' Gitta had either already told her mum about the new hire or her mum had good hearing.

Gitta sighed. 'Must everyone know our business?' She asked the question of the air, rather than her mother. Huffing in frustration, she turned to face him. 'We owe the Kochs some money. They intend to take part ownership of the diner as repayment.'

He frowned in response. 'You borrowed money from them?' The revelation surprised him. If she knew they were the local hardmen and scumbags, why would she do something so stupid as get herself into a position of debt which they could then leverage.

'I did no such thing!' she snapped, her voice getting loud. Then she realised that she was shouting without justification and forced herself to calm. 'The Kochs set out to squeeze us out of business. All the produce we buy is local. Bacon, potatoes, flour, everything we cook with is locally produced and the Kochs either own or part own every business here, as I already told you. They started pushing prices up. People who had been supplying us for years were suddenly more expensive. They were apologetic but their hands were tied. So we tried to shop elsewhere, but the nearest supermarket is more than ten kilometres away and still more expensive than we were paying. That would be manageable but the Kochs ...' she stopped speaking for a moment as she tried to form the next sentence. She wanted to lay all the blame at their door, but she didn't have the proof. 'Mum would set off but find a tree blocking the route to town. So, she would try another route and find the same problem. We couldn't prove it was them, but it was. Then the van would get mysteriously vandalised, or just wouldn't work and the repair bill at the local mechanic's would be twice what it should be. We can never both leave the diner for fear they will break in and damage something we just can't afford to repair. They were going to shut us down, so I borrowed money from Thorsten, an old friend of ours. I knew I could trust him, but it turned out he was already in debt to the Kochs himself and they bought the debt; clearing his in exchange for mine.'

'How much do you owe them?'

'Thirty thousand Euros. They don't even want it back; they are demanding a share of the business.'

'We should think ourselves lucky they don't expect the whole thing,' said her mother.

'It's worth more than that,' snapped Gitta, instantly feeling bad for her outburst. More calmly, she added. 'They want us to stay on and run it, but they want to control it like everything else around here. Now, if you will excuse me, I have to study.'

Zachary let her go, wanting to ask more but seeing that she was tired and in no mood to answer questions. He turned to her mother. 'I'm Zachary.'

'Think you'll be here long?' she asked, critical eyes examining him but not the way he saw Gitta doing when she thought he wasn't watching. Her mother, who hadn't introduced herself, was eyeing him with a degree of suspicion.

He was a little thrown by her overt hostility now that her daughter was no longer present. But he answered her question honestly. 'No probably not.'

'Didn't think so. You work for the Kochs, right? That little display during breakfast was just to throw my daughter off the scent, wasn't it? You're the hired muscle to make sure we play along and Gitta bought right into it.'

It was a straight-out accusation but though she couldn't be more wrong, he understood where the idea came from. Even though he had a natural inclination to say something funny, he dismissed all the zinging one-liners and tried to put her at ease. 'I can assure you that is not the case. I expect to be here long enough to prove that, at least.'

She snorted in disbelief but kept her eyes locked on his. 'I guess we shall see.' She turned to leave, and as she headed for the back door, drawing a cigarette from a pack as she went, she called out, 'You can call me Meg. Don't sleep with my daughter.' The door closed before he could lie that the thought had never crossed his mind.

Suddenly he was alone in the diner. He had a room and a job and there was a woman he was interested in. There were plenty of reasons to stay, but right now, the greatest of them was the sense of imbalance he felt here.

He knew that the wise move would be to pick up his backpack and start walking. He already knew that he wouldn't though. There was something troubling about this village, like a festering wound that wouldn't heal, and he was going to pick at it until he worked out how to fix it.

Chapter 6

In a hospital in Bredebo, Denmark, Jungs Potente had a room to himself, his medical insurance covering all the bills as he recovered. Mostly he was bored. He hated hospitals, avoiding them even when his family members ended up staying for any reason. There was nothing to do, he always found. Television bored him and he despised reading.

Dozing on and off with the television playing something banal to itself, he awoke when the set was turned off. Expecting a nurse, he was surprised to find two men in his room. They both wore suits but had the air of men who usually wore uniforms. They were both in their late twenties he guessed and looked like they were military. Their hair was neatly cut down to tiny stubs, the same two-millimetre length all over and they had the lean, muscular look of men who spent a lot of time practising how to hurt other men.

'What do you want?' he asked, wondering if they were police here to accuse him. None of his men would have talked and the old couple at the farm hadn't seen his face, he was certain of that.

The man nearest the door made sure it was closed. Then stepped in front of the window so no one could see in and anyone attempting entry would find the door jammed against his feet. Concern rising, Potente stammered, 'Who are you?' Then he tried to sit up so he would look more imposing, but the resultant wave of pain from his shoulder and nausea that followed forced him to slump back down on his bed. He reached for the call button to summon a nurse: he needed more pain meds.

The man nearest him snatched the cable away.

Through worried eyes, Potente watched. Neither man had spoken yet.

The nearer man looked about calmly, spotted a chair and pulled it closer before sitting on it. Only then, did he begin to speak. 'Last night, you were attacked by a werewolf.'

'I had legitimate reason to be at that farm,' Potente scrambled for a defensive position. But the man just held up a hand to quell him.

'I have no interest in your nefarious activities, Mr Potente. You survived an attack by a werewolf, and I need to talk to you about that, nothing else.'

A sudden panicked thought stampeded through Potente's brain. 'Oh, my God. Am I going to become a werewolf?' The man at the door smirked and looked at the floor.

'No,' said the seated man. 'That's not how it works. Your wounds will heal, your doctor assures me, and you will suffer no side effects other than some interesting scars and a story no one else will believe.'

Unsure whether to believe them, he felt forced to challenge the seated man's reassurances. 'But…'

The man held up his hand. 'You are about to tell me about all the werewolf films you have seen where a person survives a bite and then turns into a werewolf themselves, yes?' He sought an answer in Potente's eyes before continuing. 'You will just have to take my word for it that Hollywood have it wrong. If you are particularly worried, we can kill you now so that you will not transform and kill everyone you know.'

Potente's eyes widened at the suggestion. Over by the door, the man there was still smirking.

'I shall assume that is not what you want, Mr Potente,' said the seated man, now starting to sound bored. 'Now, perhaps you can tell me about your encounter.'

An hour later, when the two men left, Potente realised they hadn't told him who they were at any point. They knew who he was; they seemed to know all about him, but whenever he had even tried to ask a question, the seated man deftly batted it away.

Whoever they were, they were going to the farm next. They hadn't said it, but he thought they planned to catch the beast. Silently, he wished them luck, but he didn't really care what happened, so long as he never saw that thing again.

Chapter 7

Like Gitta suggested, Zachary picked the larger of the two rooms, picking up the belongings that were in it; some clothes, a few CDs and a few other possessions, and moved them all to the smaller room. The bed wasn't long enough, but he had got used to sleeping on beds far too small a long time ago by simply not doing so. He tended to sleep on the floor, putting the mattress down and using a cushion or pillows or rolled up clothes for the end where his feet went. That's what he did now, and then, because he didn't have a lot else that he needed to do, he stretched out on it and thought about going to sleep.

Then he remembered why he came here in the first place. The incident with Hans and the subsequent desire to see what that was about had made him forget, but no sooner than he got comfortable on the mattress than he was up again and heading out the door.

He was going to look into the possibility that there was a shifter here.

The diner was quiet, and he made as little noise as possible letting himself out. The back door had a key on a hook next to it, so he locked up again and took it with him. One direction was as good as any other, so he went back to the road he crossed a few hours ago to get to the diner. On the opposite side and back through the woods he would find the old abandoned garrison. He doubted there was much to see in that direction and he needed to bump into people to talk to, so he flipped a mental coin, turned left and then went right because he believed doing things on a coin toss was foolish.

There were buildings visible in both directions, farmhouses for sure with the expected barns and silos made from brick or sheet metal or possibly asbestos depending on how old the structures were. He walked for half an hour, the breeze tugging at his hair but not carrying any moisture on it thankfully despite the clouds overhead.

As soon as he saw people, he jumped a fence and started walking directly across a field to get to them. They saw him coming, he was hard to miss, not least because he wore a white t-shirt.

'Aren't you cold?' asked a woman who looked to be in her sixties. She wore a thick shawl about her head and shoulders and a coat besides plus jeans which looked to have a pair of leggings beneath them.

'Not at all,' he replied with a smile. His arrival attracted several other people who were working nearby, the chance for conversation with an odd-looking stranger sufficient to cause an impromptu break as they drifted closer. They were planting potatoes by hand.

'Isn't it a little early for potatoes?' he asked, making conversation while he waited for the stragglers to get to him.

'They're earlies,' the old woman replied, clearly believing that was explanation enough.

Waiting, because he wanted to ask his real question once when everyone was in earshot, he asked another potato related question. 'Isn't it a bit labour intensive, planting them by hand? Aren't there machines you could use?'

This time his question was fielded by a man. He looked a bit like a potato himself, Zachary observed; several warts on his face looking like tubers beginning to grow. 'There are, young man, you are quite correct. The owners will not fork out for them though and were they to do so, half of us would be out of jobs.'

'Now then,' the old woman with the shawl addressed him, 'what is it you really wanted to ask us? I don't think you walked all the way across this field to ask us about potatoes.'

Zachary couldn't help but smile; he liked the no-nonsense approach country folk often took. Flipping his eyebrows, he said, 'I've taken a job at the diner, the one run by Gitta.'

'It's the only one for kilometres, lad,' chuckled the old man.

'I start in the bar tonight so I thought I would learn some more about the area I am staying in – I'm on a gap year from university, and I stumbled across a report of a wolf hunt here last year. It made it sound like the villagers were chasing a werewolf.' He chuckled when he said it but had a sea of stony faces staring back at him as if still waiting for him to ask his question. He bit down his smile and asked, 'Was there any truth to it?'

No one said anything for a moment and a couple of them exchanged glances, but the man who looked like a potato said, 'That was a load of old cobblers, son.' Then he tutted and turned away, the potatoes more interesting than Zachary, it seemed.

His answer told him that there had been something though. If he hadn't known anything about it, his answer would have shown that. Instead, the potato man said it was a load of cobblers.

Turning to the old lady with the shawl, the only other person to have spoken, he asked, 'Can you tell me more about it? Did someone see something?'

He got a bored expression from her. Everyone was choosing to go back to planting their potatoes, but she gave him a parting word of advice. 'You should talk to Gruber. He was the one who said he saw it. He would just love to tell you all about it.'

'Gruber?' Zachary repeated. 'Where can I find him please? Where does he work?'

Her voice drifted back, 'He doesn't work. He's the local idiot.' She was already bent over poking holes in the ground with a tool and dropping potatoes into the holes from a bucket by her feet. Make a hole, drop a potato, walk backward a step, repeat.

Zachary left her to it. This was already beginning to feel like another dead end; a pointless waste of his time. There were other werewolves, meeting Zuzanna in Bremen had proved that, but he had to accept that he was a rare breed. Not for the first time, he wondered about widening his search, maybe trying America. They made all the werewolf movies after all, maybe that was because Hollywood was plagued by them.

A yawn split his face and made his decision about what to do next easy. He had slept in the cab of the truck as he escaped Denmark, but it was the kind of broken, poor-quality sleep one always gets sitting up. Zachary figured it was worse for him because he just didn't fit anywhere. On coaches he had seen women, significantly smaller than him in every way, curl up into little balls on their chairs and sleep for hours. He couldn't even get close to that if he had an empty seat next to him, which he often did because no one wants to sit next to the giant whose shoulders take up a space and a half.

He walked back to the diner, let himself in with the key he took, placed it back where he found it and went upstairs where he fell into a dreamless sleep.

Chapter 8

A light knocking noise woke him, his eyes snapping open to a darkened room. Outside the window in his room, the sun was setting. He didn't have a clock to tell the time by, but it felt like five o'clock.

The light knocking came again, a little more insistent this time.

'Hello?' he called in the darkness, sitting up and scratching his head.

From behind the door a voice replied. 'It's Gitta. It's just before five, do you want to eat before you start your shift?'

Now that sounded like a good idea. He called back, 'I'll be right down,' and clambered to his feet, stretching his arms to touch the ceiling as he worked out the kinks in his back.

Two minutes later with his teeth clean and his jeans and boots on, he went out the door with a fresh white t-shirt in his hand. He needed to do some laundry; his transient nature made it more practical to keep minimal belongings which necessitated laundry every few days.

Zachary figured he could ask her about that later, but she was in the upper hallway when he went out of the door, his t-shirt still bunched in one hand.

Gitta had been on her way to the kitchen to help her mother with final prep when she realised she left her phone upstairs in her bedroom. Going back up, she ran straight into the hulking new barman, who was somehow bigger than she remembered as if her brain had convinced itself he couldn't possibly be that big. His biceps were huge; almost like beer kegs and his shoulders were so broad she had to wonder how he found clothes to fit him. Not only that, he was ripped, his skin taut against the muscle beneath to show every lump and bump and vein.

'Everything alright?' he asked, breaking her train of thought.

She whipped her head and eyes up to look at his face, which was grinning down at her as if he knew something. 'Yes,' she murmured. 'I forgot my phone.'

Nonchalantly, he unfolded his t-shirt and pulled it on slowly, making sure his abs were tight as he rolled it down. He had seen a guy do exactly the same thing on a Coke commercial once but as he did it, he doubted he managed the same effect without the music playing. When he looked back up at her, he expected to find her staring at him or maybe biting her lip, but she looked mad instead.

'My mother thinks you are a spy employed by the Kochs. She thinks you are here to ruin the business. I told her they don't have the brain for a strategy that complex, but she also said you would try to seduce me and here you are showing off your body. What is it that you think is going to happen here, Zachary?'

Showing off his intellect he manged to say, 'Um.'

'You're still here because I want to prove to my mother that I can run this place, but if I get the slightest hint that you are working against me, you'll be out on your ear so fast your arse will singe.'

Again, the suggestion that he was working for the Kochs. He had a feeling that was going to get straightened out soon enough. For now, he said, 'Understood, boss lady.'

He was dressed and ready and she had said her piece. He wasn't sure he believed her words matched her actions, but he would gain nothing by arguing now. He thought she was attractive, and he could hope for something to occur, his life didn't provide many opportunities for intimacy, but he wouldn't actively pursue it, not when he knew he would only be here for a few days or weeks.

As she walked off to get her phone, he took himself downstairs to look for the promised dinner.

Chapter 9

Dinner turned out to be steak and potatoes and plenty of green veg. It was served buffet style, so he ate his fill, the cost of the meal deducted from his wage which suited him just fine. Meg's earlier hostility had dwindled, perhaps because she was too busy to pick a fight and perhaps because they had customers within earshot.

He chowed down and fired his dirty plate through the hatch behind the counter, then washed his hands and went to the bar where Gitta was setting up. The bar itself looked like it was hewn from a single piece of wood about a century ago. It was five metres long and accessed from one end where a gap led through to a door which in turn led to the storeroom where more bottles and fresh kegs were located.

Just as he arrived behind the bar, two men were arriving in front of it. Neither looked like they had seen a dentist in their entire lives and their skin was haggard from years spent outside though he estimated them both to be in their mid to late forties.

'What'll it be gents?' he asked, settling into the role easily.

'Two wheat beers, please,' requested the one on the left, looking Zachary up and down.

'You working here now?' asked his companion.

Zachary turned and ducked down to take two half litre bottles of wheat beer from a glass-fronted refrigerator against the back wall. He memorised where everything was kept earlier and noted that Gitta looked impressed as he stood back up.

He used a thumb to open the bottles, flicking the caps off just as Gitta produced a bottle opener from her pocket. Both men and Gitta were staring at him.

'Problem?' he asked, checking with Gitta mostly.

'Only that those bottles don't open like that. Everyone else has to use a tool.'

'Yeah,' said the farm hand on the left, 'how'd you do that?'

It became a topic of conversation quickly, men ordering more beers than they normally would just to see the big man behind the bar open each bottle with his thumbnail. Zachary had opened bottles this way ever since he could remember and thought nothing of it. Out here in a rural community, where someone spotting an albino rat would get them talking for a week, his party trick was enough to have the locals calling their family to come down and see it.

Gitta was happy, commenting that the bar had never been fuller just as another load of farmers came in. She went over to greet them, giving them the friendly treatment so they might come back more often.

The mood was light, and the crowd was getting to standing room only when a hush began to descend. It started at the door and spread across the room as more and more people stopped chatting to the person next to them.

Then the crowd started to part, no one wanting to be in the way of the men making their way to the bar. They were led by a big man, at least, he was big by the standards of the room, but still tiny when compared to Zachary. Just to his right and slightly behind was Hans, the man from this morning and there were three more besides, all bearing a distinct family resemblance: the Koch brothers. He knew their names now - one of the men at the bar filled him in earlier when Gitta was collecting glasses. Horst was the eldest at around forty-five, Zachary guessed, and always the spokesperson. He met Hans already but then there was Rolf, Peter, and Manfred. Rolf was the good looking one with the trimmed beard. His looks were fading now that he was in his late thirties, but the description made him easy to identify as they advanced. Peter was the youngest at perhaps twenty-two, and also the smallest, lacking the muscle his brothers possessed. That left Manfred who he could identify simply because he wasn't any of the others.

The room was deathly silent by the time they reached the bar.

'What'll it be gents?' asked Zachary, believing he knew where this was going but doing his best to avoid it being him that took it there.

Four of the five men facing him looked confident and in control. Skulking towards the back, Peter looked like he wanted to be somewhere else. The four were making eye contact with as many of the patrons as possible, staring them down to make them avert their eyes. Peter kept his own eyes down, trying hard to not make eye contact with anyone.

Zachary took all that in and more, noting that they all looked like they could handle themselves. All, that is, except the youngest.

Horst spoke, 'I believe you owe my brother an apology.'

'I don't want any trouble in here, Horst,' snapped Gitta, her face red and her expression already angry.

'Then you shouldn't have employed him,' raged Hans, his voice rising as he lost his cool.

Horst held up a hand to quieten his brother, a flicker of annoyance playing across his features at his brother's outburst. 'I believe that was the advice given,' Horst agreed.

Keeping her own voice calm, Gitta replied, but a tremble crept in nevertheless, 'What I do in my own establishment, is no concern of yours, Horst. Or your brother's. I will employ whomever I wish.'

'Nevertheless, I believe it would have been for the best if you had listened to the advice Hans gave. This is our town, Gitta. You would be best to remember that since we shall shortly be business partners.'

That was the comment that unravelled her calm. 'You're not getting this bar!' she shouted, playing right into his hands as he smiled at the little lost girl trying to play in the man's world he perceived.

'You have two days to come up with thirty thousand Euros, Gitta. Perhaps you should calm down and we can discuss how the new system of management will work.'

'Never,' she replied quietly.

Zachary was bored already and felt like throwing them out. It had been a pleasant evening so far, the locals all having a great time and not a single negative emotion had been shared until these five clowns walked in. He placed one hand on the bar and vaulted it easily, landing in the gap right in front of Horst. 'If you're not drinking, and you don't plan to be friendly, I'm afraid I will have to escort you out, gentlemen.'

Horst just smiled at him and turned around. 'Everyone out. Now.' There was a pause of about a second before the sound of the first beer bottle being put down was heard, but it was followed by more and more, as with a barely audible murmur, the crowd in the bar moved toward the door, abandoning their drinks to obey Horst's instruction.

Gitta was quivering with rage. 'Damn you, Horst. Damn you all. You don't own those people.'

He turned around once more so he was facing Zachary but walked around to his side so he could lean on the bar and show how relaxed he was feeling. 'Oh, but I do, Gitta. Every single one of them either works for me directly or owes me money or knows I have the controlling interest in their business. Like I said, this is my town.' Telling everyone to leave was a revolting display of power, something Zachary had rallied against his entire life, but never had he seen anyone with such a complete grip on a place.

Hans and his brothers all came to the bar, Hans making sure he locked eyes with Zachary to scowl at him on his way by. Peter trailed along behind, following because he had no choice, Zachary thought.

Taking a handful of peanuts from a bowl on the bar, Horst said, 'I think, since it's so quiet in here, my brothers and I will stop for a drink. Five beers, please. On the house, of course, being as how you owe me thirty thousand Euros and I'm not even charging you interest.'

Gitta felt utterly defeated. She had no idea how she was ever going to come up with the money, the bank had already refused, but she wasn't going to bow down, no matter what. 'You can go to hell, Horst.'

'Five beers,' he repeated. 'Now.' His final word carried all manner of threat with it and for Zachary it was the greenlight.

His beast was trying to rise, it could feel the anger bubbling inside him, and it wanted to be free. He couldn't shift here though and was fighting hard to suppress the desire to become what he wanted to be. The effort of staying his current shape had already made him twitchy and Horst's threat took him to the edge.

'I think we should all go outside,' he said, his voice flat and firm. 'You are being impolite.' Zachary had killed before. Not that it was something he was proud of or ever wanted to do again, but if there were people in the world who deserved to die, then he was talking to one of them right now.

'Yes,' agreed Horst to Zachary's surprise. 'I think we should escort you to the autobahn where you can continue on your journey. There's nothing for you here but trouble and pain.'

This worked even better. Zachary wanted to be well away from Gitta's bar when he transformed.

Wordlessly, he started toward the door, motioning for the Kochs to follow. This was going to be fun.

'No!' shouted Gitta, running after him.

Zachary turned around but continued walking backward. 'I'll be right back, babe.' He flashed a big smile. He was genuinely looking forward to this. Getting them to go with him had been so easy and now he could face off against all five of them and give them a light beating. He wouldn't even use his claws. They could return tomorrow blathering stories about how he was a werewolf, but no one would have seen it, and no one would believe them. Zachary would deny everything and make sure they came off looking cowardly and weak. He also liked how Gitta looked so concerned for him right now. He hadn't intended to call her babe and he saw the flicker of annoyance dance across her face. Too late to take it back now though.

Gitta knew she had to stop them. They would kill him, that was what she believed. She wanted to report it when her last barman said the wrong thing and vanished in the night, but there was no evidence and the locals would never turn on the Kochs; too terrified of repercussions to ever stand up to them. There was something about Zachary's confidence though. He genuinely had no fear so either he was truly stupid, or he knew something she didn't.

They were going out the door already, Zachary leading the way as if he couldn't wait to get started. She had to follow – they wouldn't hurt him bad if she was there. As Peter Koch glanced at her, his eyes flicking up from the ground just for a split second, she caught how sad he looked and that made up her mind.

As their truck engines fired and a slew of gravel shot out from the back tyres, Gitta was already snatching up the keys to her mother's van.

'You can't go after them.' Her mother was blocking her path, but Gitta wasn't to be dissuaded.

'They'll kill him,' she argued, shoving past her mother to get to the door.

Even as Meg shouted for her to stop, her heart sunk. The van was there but it had four flat tyres. The Kochs knew what they were doing and how to make sure no one interfered. Feeling defeated, Gitta snarled at the night air.

'There's nothing you can do now,' her mother said softly. Standing behind her daughter and ready to comfort her. 'Paula is upstairs. You should go to her. If you go after him, they'll kill you both, Gitta. That's what they'll do. Horst doesn't care about the law; he thinks he can't be touched. He might even be right.'

Gitta said nothing, nodding her agreement. She would inflate the tyres in the morning, but she was still going after the Kochs as soon as her mother wasn't watching.

Chapter 10

Outside the bar on the gravel and dirt yard, were two large Mercedes pickup trucks. They were the only two vehicles outside so Zachary headed right for them, jumping in the rear of the first one he came to.

If they had truly planned to take him out to the autobahn they would have sent him to get his things but Zachary felt certain they were going to drive him somewhere remote where they planned to either kill him, or just give him a good enough beating that he wouldn't come back. They would probably feel confident enough about leaving him alive. If he called the cops, the entire village would testify that the Kochs were somewhere else when the alleged incident occurred such was their grip on the village.

The Kochs were all riding in the cabs, each truck was the variant with the crew cab that could seat five easily, so it was two in one and two in the other plus the youngest brother riding in the back of the pickup which Zachary was sitting in the back of.

He felt calm as the pickup bounced along the road, the potholes jolting the suspension every few metres. The youngest brother turned around to sneak a peek at Zachary only once. What he saw was the giant man staring back at him and looking serene. It should have worried him. Maybe it did, Zachary thought, but his brothers wouldn't show any fear so neither did he. He looked away though, focusing his eyes back on the road ahead and after a while Zachary turned his own eyes to watch the black trees going by.

On the road that ran in front of the diner, they drove at a pace of about eighty kilometres an hour until they began to slow ten minutes later. Each driver turned off his lights before they turned off the road. Just as Zachary expected they were in the middle of nowhere, going down a dirt track into a copse of trees. He could see well enough, his night vision attuned to the dark now that he had been outside for several minutes. When he shifted, he would have perfect vision, but he held off for now, curious to see what they had planned for him.

Once both cars were through the first line of trees and out of sight from the road, they stopped. Zachary jumped over the side of the truck's flatbed in one smooth move, then walked a couple of paces so the men would exit and face him on a single front.

The Koch brothers had taken him to a clearing, light from the moon illuminating it so he could easily see their faces as they climbed out. They looked calm and relaxed, ready for what they planned to do. All apart from the youngest. His eyes rarely left the ground, which gave Zachary the impression he was here under duress.

Horst looked at Zachary, chuckling to himself, 'You are one confident S.O.B. You know that? There's five of us and you're standing there like you are going to beat us.'

Zachary allowed a grin to play across his face and pulled off his t-shirt. He might not even need to change for this. If he could hold the beast at bay by tricking himself into just coming at this like it was a bit of fun, then maybe he could hand out some lumps in human form.

He took a step forward, not bothering with conversation in his plan to get the task done. Afterward, he would take one of their trucks to go back to the bar. And who knows? Maybe he would hang around the village for a while and see how the brothers acted after a lesson in humility.

Horst held up a hand, begging Zachary for a moment's grace. Then to Zachary's great surprise, they too started taking off their upper layer of clothes. All five brothers stripped down to expose their chests until they too were standing outside in the frigid late winter air in just jeans and boots.

Zachary scratched his head and held up a hand to stop them. 'If this a big gay thing then ... I'm cool with you being gay, but I'm not joining in. So you can put your shirts back on and, well ... whatever.'

Again, Horst smiled, a laugh teasing the corners of his mouth. 'This is where you get to find out how little you know about the world.'

Zachary was genuinely curious, his desire to find out what Horst was on about enough to give him pause.

Then, Horst touched his left forearm with his right hand, repeating the motion on his right forearm with his left hand. Two glowing marks appeared on his skin, like tattoos hidden beneath the surface had just been activated. 'You see,' said Horst, as more glowing marks appeared on his upper arms and across his chest and shoulders. 'We are unlike anyone you have ever faced before, big man. Your confidence comes from believing you are big enough to beat us. You have probably won a lot of fights in your life. Today though, your size and strength are of no consequence.' Then he moved his hands, a strong pulse of air slamming into Zachary to shove him backwards.

Caught out by the unexpected show of ... what? Magic? Zachary's feet snagged on a root and he fell, sprawling in the dirt much to his chagrin. The tattoos were appearing all over the other men's arms and upper bodies when he looked again. They appeared to be symbols, each carefully drawn and the same on each man.

He had never seen anything like this before. He knew about magic sure enough, meeting Otto the wizard not very long ago and demons shortly thereafter. The demons were able to fling around some serious firepower and the wizard was able to control elements; air, water, earth, and with them conjure spells that could do all manner of damage. Otto didn't have these tattoos though. At least, Zachary didn't think he did. Trawling his memory now, he couldn't think of a time when he had seen him with his shirt off. Whatever the case, he hadn't expected the Kochs to be able to wield magic, if that was what was about to happen, but his confidence at being able to beat them hadn't dipped. He was immortal, or something like that, but further pondering on what they might be able to do was neither necessary nor possible because it was fighting time.

The five men fanned out, advancing toward him as he kicked off his boots and undid his jeans. The brothers exchanged glances, wondering what the large man was doing as he carefully folded his jeans and placed them on top of his boots. He was naked suddenly, an odd thing to do unless he was somehow accepting his fate and going back to his maker the same way he arrived.

Paying no heed to the brothers, Zachary stretched out his arms and let the transformation start. If he focused, he could force it to happen in a little more than a second. However, he took his time tonight, enjoying the Kochs' confident expressions melt away as he grew in height and girth and his skin hardened to become almost impenetrable. His werewolf form was by far his favourite, he rarely changed into anything else, even though he could.

The Kochs were dazed for a heartbeat, rooted to the spot as the man's body and face began to warp and change. Then, a shout from Rolf broke the reverie as he conjured fire and threw it at their intended victim.

So it is magic, Zachary acknowledge. It was different to how Otto did it and far less powerful than the spells the demons threw around. He took the time to casually look down at the fire hitting his belly and lower chest before looking back up at the Kochs. Then he smiled, making sure he showed them a lot of teeth. 'Don't worry, chaps,' he said. 'I won't bite you. I don't want to get Koch in my mouth.'

'What the hell is that?' cried Peter, terrified by the apparition. He hadn't wanted to be part of this. He never did, yet he felt he was more trapped than the people living in the village under his brothers' boots. His ability with the magic was the weakest because he didn't really want to do it. Backing away from the horror before him, his feet moving of their own volition, he stumbled forward again when Hans shoved him hard in the back.

'Fight!' Hans roared in his face as he too, conjured fire and threw it at the monster.

The flames were a nuisance to Zachary, but little more. They warmed his skin pleasantly as they singed the coarse hair covering his body, the intensity far too weak to do any lasting damage.

It had gone on long enough, he decided, flexing his broad shoulders to raise his arms. Each hand ended with five razor sharp claws which he showed them now, extending his fingers one at a time for effect as he straightened to his full two and half metre height to tower over them by an even greater margin.

Remembering Horst's words, he spoke, his voice now an even deeper grumbling bass rumble than it had been before, 'Now this is where you get to find out how little *you* know about the world.'

Then he lunged.

He didn't want to kill them, not because he thought they deserved to live, but because he didn't want to think of himself as the judge and jury. It wasn't his role in life, but he could hurt them badly enough to make them amend their ways.

The first to get it was Hans. He was closest and Zachary already didn't like him. A giant foot to the man's midriff doubled him over, exposing his neck, which Zachary clubbed with his right elbow. It was a kindness, he considered, given what he could have done. Hans collapsed to the ground, his face slamming into the dirt. Horst was right on him though, conjuring the air to shunt him sideways.

Zachary stumbled, and was caught again by Rolf before he could recover. This time the pulse of air knocked him over so for the second time, he ended up sat on his butt.

Now he was getting mad. Doing his best to avoid hurting them wasn't working, the remaining four were combining their attack to keep him off balance. Horst hit him with fire again, more intense this time though it was still too weak to have much impact. Then, Rolf joined in, fire and air now buffeting him from three different sides as they tried to keep him pinned in place and burn him to death.

Hans hadn't moved since he hit the dirt and Zachary could see the youngest brother was going through the motions - doing the spell but having no effect with it. He was the weak link so there was little point in focusing on him. If he took out one more of the three remaining brothers, he was confident their ability to do anything to stop him would be lost.

Choosing a target, Zachary gripped the soil with his toes and thrust upwards and out-wards, heading for Horst. Their leader saw him coming but couldn't get out of the way before a slashing hand ripped through the skin of his chest, carving down to the bone of his ribs.

A sickening scream of pain echoed across the landscape and Horst fell backwards, the spell in his hand failing as he stared disbelievingly down at his chest. Blood flowed, but Zachary was already turning to his next target, the good-looking one, Rolf. Rolf had some muscle, more than any of his brothers, but nothing compared to Zachary.

Like Horst, he saw the werewolf coming but could do nothing to get out of the way. Foolishly he tried to fend off the attack, switching his spell to create a pulse of air that might deflect the monster. However, it was too weak and too hastily conjured to have any hope of stopping the beast surging his way. Realising he could not avoid the blow coming, Rolf raised an arm to parry the werewolf at the last moment.

What Zachary saw was an easy target, the foolish man raising an arm as if he wanted it cut off. He could probably have achieved that with one chopping motion, but he turned his hand and drove the claws through the arm instead, skewering it with four fingers before sweeping the man's legs.

As Rolf fell away, his mouth forming a silent O of excruciating pain too terrible to permit sound, Zachary wheeled around, spinning off one foot to face the remaining two. He leered at them now as they both backed away.

The youngest brother looked about ready to wet himself, the other, Manfred, also looked terrified now that three of his brothers were out of the fight, but he was still fumbling with his hands as he tried to conjure some new spell that might save him.

He didn't need to be saved; Zachary decided enough damage had been done.

Glancing around to quickly assess the wounded brothers' condition, he decided they would all live. Even Hans was moving again, getting off lightly with some bruising and a headache. It was time to deliver a message. 'Right, you bunch of Kochs. Here's how it is going to be. I don't ever expect to see any of you ever again. I'll be hanging around here for a while to make sure you pack up and leave. Take your business elsewhere, leave these people in peace. Or next time I won't be so friendly.'

'This is our town,' growled Horst through his pain. 'We own it. It's ours.'

Zachary stalked across to him, three easy loping paces to cross the distance making sure his claws were visible. Horst tried to wriggle back, but Zachary stood on his left leg to pin him in place. Then he crouched and placed his right knee on the ground. 'I don't care, Horst. You cannot hope to hurt me, there is no chance you can beat me. I am a drifter who can kill you all and move on without the slightest care. Get in your truck, lick your wounds and drive until morning. If I see you again, I'll kill you.'

It was an empty threat. He wouldn't kill them. But they didn't know that, and they had every reason to believe that he could and would.

He lingered over Horst for a few seconds, staring down at him to maintain eye contact. What he saw was anger and defiance, but when Zachary broke off and looked at the brothers, he saw defeat and fear. They would go, he was sure of it, but he would stay for a while just to be sure.

Turning his back on all of them as a display of confidence, Zachary walked back over to his pile of clothes where he waited. Slowly, the younger brothers helped the wounded back to their feet, carrying them or supporting them across the clearing to the cars. The injuries necessitated a switch around of drivers, but the engines roared to life, the mechanical sounds somehow alien and out of place in the dark and quiet of the night. Headlights flashed to life, casting blinding beams across the landscape.

As they circled around and drove back down the narrow dirt track away from the clearing and back through the copse of trees, Zachary realised his mistake.

'Shit,' he swore. 'I should have got a lift back to the diner.'

Chapter 11

The ten-minute drive out to the clearing in the woods took more than an hour to walk back. Zachary shifted back to human form and dressed again before he started walking, following the route the cars took until he reached the road and then turned right to head back to the diner.

His shifter nature hadn't imbued him with any special sense of direction or ability to navigate by smell. He was just a vanilla human when in human form. Well, vanilla with a side order of very big, very strong, virtually impervious to cold and heat and able to take a lot of punishment.

With nothing to distract him on the walk back to the diner, Zachary's thoughts turned to his supernatural nature. Would he have grown so big were it not for the beast within him? His parents were nothing like his size, his father topping out at just a shade over one metre eighty, though he had shrunk a little by the time Zachary was a teenager and eclipsing him.

His parents were still alive, but he had no contact with them. He got the impression his father wanted nothing to do with him. They fell out a lot when he was a teenager. It wasn't so much that he was headstrong or disobedient. He just kept getting into trouble and his father was always on the side of the police, refusing ever to believe what Zachary told him even though it was the truth.

'Hey kid, you think you're tough?' That was the sort of sentence he heard all the time because he would step in to stop a bully picking on someone. Another one was, 'I'm gonna kick your ass.' When he heard words like that he always figured the person either meant it, in which case they were just about to attack him, or they were trying to see if he was a coward which was a green light to show them he wasn't.

He got into a lot of fights because he would stick his nose in where other people didn't want it. Over the years he came to recognise different types of people. There were sheep; the type of people who wanted an easy life and would move out of the way rather than stand up for themselves unless they absolutely had to. Then there were wolves. There were far fewer wolves than there were sheep which was a good thing because they would circle the sheep and pick on them. Not just physically like a childhood bully in the playground, but mentally, financially, psychologically. Zachary saw people work other people to the bone because they wanted to be rich and were happy to make their money through the tears of others. These injustices made his blood boil, but then he was neither a sheep nor a wolf. Zachary was a sheepdog. He possessed a natural instinct to protect the herd. It wasn't even his herd.

When he first felt the change coming over him at puberty, Zachary had already worked out the sheepdog thing so it struck him as laughably ironic that he could now alter his form to be a wolf if he so chose. He had no idea where his ability came from and watched his parents for weeks, curious to see if either of them ever went out in the middle of the night to run around as a wolf or anything else. He got no indication there was anything special about them though. Special: that was what he told himself he was. Zachary changed if he wanted to, which was almost always for fun, but just once or twice because he wanted to really, really scare someone.

The worst part was that his size intimidated people. You might think this a good thing, but men don't like to be intimidated by a boy so they would make themselves feel better by threatening him. Seeing his age, they would assume they could scare him off, but think back to the bit about them giving him a green light.

With the rage, the change got harder to control, the beast within slipping out when he fought, even when he tried to keep a lid on it. By the time he turned seventeen he was known to the local police and tired of fighting with his father. In the dead of night, he packed a bag and left home. His decision to leave for his father's safety more than anything else; he would never forgive himself if the old man pushed him too hard one night and Zachary hurt him.

His thoughts were interrupted by a movement to his right. There was something in the bushes; something trying to stay very, very still. He wasn't going to say, 'Who's there?' It would just sound ridiculous. Instead he charged forward, his intention to scare whatever was in there into giving away its position.

Nothing moved.

Wanting to trust his senses, which assured him there was something there, he squinted into the dark for most of a minute before accepting that he must have imagined it. He still had a long walk back to the diner yet and he wanted to have a beer before bed. The clock in his head told him it couldn't be any later than eleven o'clock, so he set off again, the moonlight creating a shadow in front of him as he walked down the centre of the road.

Behind him, a shadow detached itself from a tree and watched as he walked away.

Chapter 12

A speck of light in the distance became a square of light and then a window in the upper floor of the diner. His thoughts had drifted back to his childhood and his mother and about how he would most likely never see his parents again, but Zachary pushed the walk down memory lane from his mind as he approached the building; it was time to get some sleep.

His hope to sneak inside and crawl onto his mattress was ruined by finding all the doors locked. He told himself he shouldn't be surprised but knocked as gently as he thought he could get away with, increasing the volume after a minute of waiting and another minute later bashing it with a fist.

'Hey, Gitta! Meg! Let me in. It's cold out here,' he added though he wasn't cold at all.

When Zachary left with the Koch brothers, Gitta suffered a wave of guilt that made her feel nauseous. They were going to beat him half to death, she knew. Or worse maybe. It was her fault. Her sense of pride, her stubbornness made her push back against Horst and Hans and the others when she knew no good could come of it.

She didn't know the man, but he had taken a job in her business and that made him her responsibility. Now he was going to pay for her mistakes and there was nothing she could do about it. But no sooner had she thought that than she started to argue with herself. She could do something about it, she could follow them in her mother's van and prevent them hurting him.

Of course, her mother had tried to stop her, but she needn't have bothered because the Kochs had already disabled the van. Her heart had sunk in defeat, not because she was attracted to him, though he did have some alluring qualities such as his almost constant smile and ability to make her, and most other people laugh. He was back though, hammering on her door and his voice sounded strong.

She had snuck out to follow once she thought her mother was no longer listening. She saw which way they went and though that didn't mean she knew where they were, she didn't think they would leave the village boundaries. That meant no more than about five kilometres. Maybe she wouldn't find them, maybe she would. Maybe she would find him hurt and be able to help him.

What she knew was that she had to try, so that was what she was going to do, running cross country in the dark in search of a man she met this morning. But then, she saw him coming toward her, walking down the road and humming to himself. She hid, desperate that he wouldn't see her, and she watched. Had he beaten them? He was a huge specimen but surely five against one were odds too great for any man.

Once he passed her and the coast was clear, she raced back to the diner and had just got back to her bedroom and into her nightclothes when he started knocking on the door. Gitta met her mother on the upper landing, their eyes as wide as each other's as they both fumbled to get to the stairs.

Arriving downstairs with her mother on her shoulder, she flung the door open and there he was, still wearing his t-shirt and jeans and apart from a few dirty smudges on his clothes, looking wholly unscathed.

'What the hell happened?' she demanded, the cold night air swirling in around her bare legs.

Zachary opened his mouth to speak, his eyes dropping half a metre from her eyes where what he saw made his words get stuck. Then he glanced away guiltily, and she looked down to find her nipples tenting the front of the t-shirt she slept in.

Zachary had a smile on his face, he was actually chuckling to himself as he made sure he kept his eyes on neutral territory though she thought she saw him mouth the word, 'Wow.'

She couldn't help but squint her eyes at him as she snagged a coat from a peg just behind her. Pulling it on, she said, 'Is this better?' Her tone was undeniably snippy and when he looked up again, he still had the smirk on his face.

'Not really,' he admitted. 'I kinda liked how it was before,' It was a guilty admission but also the truth.

He could tell she was naked beneath the flimsy t-shirt she wore, and it didn't help that it only just covered what was necessary. If she were to reach upward, he would get a flash of something he hadn't seen in a while.

'Oh, good grief!' exclaimed Meg, watching the silent foreplay zing back and forth. 'Get inside, for goodness sake. All the warm air is escaping.'

The clock on the wall said it was coming up on midnight when he sat at a table in the bar and Gitta handed him a beer. She was having a shot of brandy, she felt she needed it. Meg left them to it, taking a shot of brandy for herself, 'To ward off the cold,' she claimed as she headed back to the stairs.

'I scared them off,' Zachary told her when she prompted him by asking what happened again. He took a swig of his beer, emptying half the contents in one go, but caught her staring at him in disbelief. He pumped a bicep, lifting one arm and contracting the muscle as he bent his arm to make the vein pop out. 'I gave them the gun show and they ran away?' he tried.

'Are they dead?' she asked, completely serious.

He couldn't tell if she thought that would be a good thing or a bad thing, but he answered honestly, dropping his arm back down to face her with a serious expression. 'No. I hurt them though. Horst and Rolf got the worst of it though Hans might have a concussion. I told them to leave or it would be worse next time.'

Her eyes were like saucers as she stared at him. 'How? I mean, I get that you are a big guy but there were five of them.'

'More like four,' he countered. 'The youngest...'

'Peter,' she filled in the blank.

'He didn't look like he wanted any part of it.'

She knew it was true. 'He and I went to school together. He's not like his brothers. He's actually kind of sweet but they won't let him be who he wants to be. They think he has to be just like them, or the community might see a sign of weakness. They stand united; that's their thing.'

He took another swig of beer. 'Well you'll be pleased to hear that he got away unscathed. The others not so much. At least two of them will need hospital treatment. You won't see them for weeks, if ever.'

'They won't leave,' she argued. They were too invested in the area. Whatever Zachary had done to them would just make them come back harder. They would... 'They will kill you,' she blurted the moment the thought reached her head. 'You don't know them. I think they killed the last barman when he argued with Horst. He just vanished one day, and they told me he decided to leave town. They'll kill you for sure though. They might even do it publicly to send a message.'

Zachary let a half smile creep onto his face. 'I'm kind of hard to kill.'

'Are you bulletproof?' she asked, snapping her question at him as her frustration overwhelmed her relief at seeing him alive and in one piece.

He tilted his head as he answered. 'Not quite.' He wasn't bulletproof but he honestly didn't believe a bullet could kill him.

She didn't know what that meant other than they were still in trouble, if not more trouble than they had been. They were injured though. That's what Zachary claimed, and she believed him. He had to have beaten them, there was no other way he could possibly be sitting here now if he hadn't.

It was all too much to deal with tonight. She hoped for a few days respite. Could she hope for more than that? Maybe if she had a few extra days she could come up with a way to get the money and pay Horst back. Zachary would have to move on and life in the village wouldn't change much because the Kochs would still be here but perhaps she could keep the business out of their hands.

'I'm going to bed,' she announced, getting up. Her untouched glass of brandy beckoned so she knocked it back in one hit, savouring the flavour and loving the feeling of warmth as it soaked through her body. 'I'll see you at breakfast. I'll need a hand, so I'll wake you at five. It's too hard working the diner all by myself.'

Zachary watched her depart, thankful her shapely bottom was hidden beneath the long coat she wore and not wiggling invitingly as she walked away from him. The rest of the beer went in one gulp, but he gave her a minute to put the coat back by the door and get upstairs and into her room before he followed. The last thing he needed was to see more of her in the flimsy t-shirt or follow her up the stairs where one glance might... well. It was just better if he waited a minute.

He noticed something as she walked away though, something that was nothing to do with how delicious she looked. He stared at it, wanting to ask her a question but she was through the door and gone, so he filed it away for another time.

Chapter 13

The following morning, he was up before anyone else in the house, heading downstairs early to make coffee and wait for them to rise. It was more than an hour before he heard them moving about above him, the sound of feet on floorboards echoing down through the old house just as the scent of fresh coffee must be reaching their noses. The coffee wasn't the only smell wafting out of the kitchen though.

'Is that bread?' asked Gitta, who told herself it couldn't be as she made her way downstairs.

On a wire cooling rack next to the oven sat two round, perfectly crisp looking loafs. She had told her nose it was lying and was now having an argument with her eyes.

'It's soda bread,' Zachary told her, offering a mug of coffee he poured as he heard her approach. 'It's really not that hard to make.'

'I know,' she replied as she took the coffee and poked the bread to make sure it was real. 'I just haven't seen a man make it before. Ever. The men around here would struggle to make a sandwich.'

'I worked in a bakery for a while,' he told her as he drained his mug and refilled it.

'Even so. Wow. What time did you get up?'

He glanced at the clock. 'Around four maybe.' She just looked at him, one eyebrow raised like he was insane. 'I like the early shift. Where do you keep the butter?'

Five minutes later the first loaf was reduced to crumbs as Zachary ate more than half of it himself, melted butter running onto the underside of his hand. Gitta and her mother, Meg, accounted for the rest of it while Zachary eyed the second loaf and wondered about bacon.

'The morning breakfast crowd will start arriving in half an hour,' Meg reminded her daughter. I need you two out so I can get on with cooking.

'Need me to do anything?' Zachary asked, doing his best to be useful. He liked it here. The initial problem that made him stay had been dealt with in less than a day so he figured he might stick around for a while. It was a quiet community and he had a job that was both easy and pleasant. He wasn't done with the shifter hunt either. That might yet yield something, so he was going to hang around for at least a little while.

Meg looked him square in the face. 'Can you peel a potato?'

Standing in the kitchen peeling potatoes and plopping them into a large pan of water gave him a chance to ask Meg a few questions. Checking over his shoulder to see if she was too busy to chat and deciding to try anyway, he said, 'I hear there was a fella here that saw a werewolf. A man by the name of Gruber.'

Meg looked across at him, continuing to fry bacon on the flat top as she squinted in his direction. 'Where did you hear that?'

'It was online. I like to read about the places I stay but didn't expect to find anything much about such a small community.'

'Yeah, well, I wouldn't give it any further thought. That's just Gruber. He's a sandwich short of a loaf.'

'But he saw something.' Zachary noted that he had asked about this twice now and both people answering him had brushed it off without denying there was a werewolf.

Meg pushed the bacon to the side and wiped her hands on her pinafore, bustling across to the other side of the kitchen and ignoring his question as if too busy to answer him. Just as he opened his mouth to prompt a reply, Gitta poked her head through the hatch.

'Can I get a hand out here, Zac?'

'I'm done here,' he announced, dropping the last potato into the pan and hefting the whole thing to the giant gas hob. The question would have to wait, but he couldn't deny the impression that Meg knew something she didn't want to share with him.

By 0559hrs there was a small but growing queue of men and woman outside the door to the diner. Inside, the diner was filled with the glorious smell of frying breakfast, smoky bacon dominating, but he could smell toast and coffee too.

Gitta opened the doors, welcoming one and all as they filed in from the dark and cold outside. The first man through the doors stopped when he saw Zachary over by the counter. It was as if he couldn't believe his eyes. The man behind him didn't see the man in front stop so bumped into him, the man behind him doing the same. It turned into a kerfuffle as they pushed each other to get inside.

Zachary was instantly the topic of conversation, some of the villagers keeping their voices low as they discussed him but an old fellow, making his way to the single service counter addressed him directly.

'I felt sure you'd be gone this morning.'

Zachary recognised him from breakfast yesterday and again from the bar last night where almost everyone now in the room had congregated before the Kochs ruined it. 'Why's that?' he asked

The old man then struggled to get his next sentence right, mumbling a few words before saying, 'Those the Kochs take a dislike to, don't tend to stay around.'

Zachary figured that was probably true. As he filled the old boy's coffee mug, he said, 'I convinced them to leave me alone.'

The man looked at Zachary's arms, the veins running over the massive muscles enough to complete the story. 'I dare say you did.'

Soon Meg was doling out heaping plates of breakfast to keep the farm workers going in the cold environment and Gitta was taking them to tables and bringing empties back with Zachary doing much the same. The diner had a pleasant rhythm to it, which was why it was so obvious to Zachary when the hum of the rhythm stopped.

Like the previous night in the bar, silence began to spread across the room, starting at the windows but sweeping swiftly across to the single diner counter and every head was facing the same way when Zachary looked up.

The Kochs were outside.

Both cars had pulled into the carpark and all five brothers were getting out.

Zachary narrowed his eyes at them as they crossed the car park. Everyone inside could see them. Even though it was dark outside, light, given off by the diner, was enough to be sure who it was he was looking at. They approached in arrowhead formation again, Horst at the tip with two brothers either side as if they rehearsed it or something.

There was no sign of any injuries.

Gitta arrived by his side. 'I guess they decided to stay. I thought you said you injured Horst and Rolf.'

He blew out a breath through his nose, a huff of disappointment as much as anything but there was some frustration in there too. What was this? He cleaved Horst's chest open just a few hours ago. He would have needed dozens of stitches to close the wounds and Rolf was bleeding terribly when they carried/dragged him to the car. There was no way they had patched them up and they were now toughing it out to make sure they were seen.

No. They had healed themselves. This had to be part of their magic. It startled him when he first saw it last night, but recent events in Bremen proved he wasn't the only supernatural around. He even saw Otto heal when he was wounded but that wasn't his magic doing it. Otto healed from terrible wounds because he got the same burst of demon juice as Zachary and it made them both immortal. Or something. It made them both something, but that something meant they healed instantly and could shrug off wounds.

Somehow the Kochs could do the same.

It was bad news. Even though their magic was no match for him, they could heal themselves and that was a problem. It made them feel, or at least, act invincible.

They reached the door and came inside, a broad smile on Horst's face as he dipped his head in Zachary's direction.

'Do you want to serve them or throw them out?' he asked Gitta. He hadn't answered her question about his claim to have injured them. He had no way of explaining how he came to inflict the injuries without telling her what he was and then she wouldn't believe him so he would have to show her and then she would scream and run away and never let him come near her again. He had made that mistake before.

Gitta grabbed a pot of coffee. 'I'll deal with them. You go help my mother in the kitchen please. I don't think it's a good idea to have you out here with them.'

He complied because he was happy enough to do so. He was going to visit the Kochs today when breakfast was over. They hadn't listened to his warning and were now flaunting their healing ability in his face. Perhaps killing them would have to be the route he took.

Gitta swallowed her pride as she approached their table. She hated them with passion; they were scum so far as she was concerned but she had little choice but to put up with them. Falling asleep last night after Zachary returned unharmed, she fantasised about the Kochs not being around for a little while. About having the time to work out how to raise more money. Yet here they were, unscathed despite Zachary's claims to have hurt them so bad they would want to leave the village.

How had he escaped then? He wasn't injured and they weren't injured. Had they had a little chat, and all got on famously, deciding to shake hands and let it go? Then it hit her. They hadn't let him go. They were all on the same side. Her mother had been right from the start!

Cursing her gullibility, she slammed the coffee pot down on the table, accidentally giving it enough force that it smashed, sending steaming hot coffee across the tabletop in every direction.

The Koch brothers all leapt up to avoid the scalding hot spill, accusing looks all directed at the petite woman.

'What the hell are you playing at, missy?' demanded Hans. His groin soaked where he hadn't been fast enough.

'I can't believe you put a spy in here. That's low even for you.' She was snarling into Horst's face though he met her eyes with a smirk.

'I have no idea what you are talking about, Gitta,' he replied calmly.

She wasn't listening though. Her attention was already on the hatch through to the kitchen. 'Hey, Zac. Get out here and join your friends,' she shouted to him.

The diner's patrons continued eating, watching the theatre like it was dinner and a show.

Zachary came around the side of the kitchen and out through the door to rejoin everyone in the diner. He heard what Gitta said but he didn't understand what she meant by it. Surely, she didn't think he was with the Kochs. He stopped halfway across the room, close enough to feel the rage sheeting off her.

'You think I am here because I work for them?' he asked, his voice filled with a disappointment he couldn't hide.

'Why are you here? she demanded. 'No one just walks into a place and asks for a job. You went with them last night but there isn't a mark on you. Or on them.'

'Yeah,' echoed the old boy at the counter.

All around the diner, the villagers could see the incongruity and were whispering to each other.

Horst saw his opportunity. 'I guess the game's up, Zac. You might as well come clean.'

Zachary was getting mad. The anger was welling inside, making the desire to change hard to control. Horst was grinning like the cat with the cream and it made Zachary want to tear his head off right in front of everyone. His shoulders were heaving up and down as he fought for control, and he closed his eyes when he felt them begin to change. Any second now they would be glowing and there was no coming back from that.

'I am not with them, Gitta,' he managed between clenched teeth. 'I am here to help.'

She didn't buy a word of it. What possible reason could there be for the lack of injuries last night and his presence here in the first place. They sent him to distract her; his mission to prevent her from getting the money together to pay off Horst or maybe to find out if she even had any money. The detail of it didn't matter.

'Just get out,' she hissed.

'We'll meet you out front, buddy,' added Horst, making matters worse as he pretended they were in it together.

Anger boiled in Zachary's veins so he did the only thing he could; he turned around and walked away. He refused to change in front of all these people and scare them half to death. Hell, the old boy at the counter might have a heart attack.

Back through the door and into the hallway behind the dining room, he opened his eyes. He knew without looking that they were glowing red and his teeth had that odd feeling where they don't quite fit his mouth. He only ever got that when the change was trying to happen and being held in check.

Wanting to scream to the sky, he thumped the wall with one mighty fist, dust in the rafters of the dining room sifting down as the whole building shook.

Gitta locked eyes with Horst. 'You can get out too. You'll not get served here.'

Chuckling, Horst picked up his car keys from a dry piece of the table. 'Come on, boys. Let's go.' They all moved toward the door, but Horst paused to look back at her. 'To-morrow, Gitta. That money is due tomorrow.'

Then they were gone, leaving her seething with half of the village seeing her humiliation. They piled into their pickups and left the parking area with a spray of dirt and gravel.

She didn't notice that they hadn't waited for Zachary. But her mother did.

Chapter 14

Their visit to the farm in Hjepsted revealed very little they didn't already know. They were on the trail of Zachary Barnabus, that much they could be sure of; everyone confirmed the picture they carried was of the man they had seen. They always arrived after he left though. The moment he exposed himself as a werewolf, he then vanished, and there was never any indication about where he might go next.

They both worked for the Supernatural Investigation Alliance though the cards they showed people claimed they worked for the Kriminal Investigation Bureau. The Supernatural Investigation Alliance, or SIA for short was a secret group, funded by the government which had quickly spread from one country to almost all others as they fought to identify and control the growing supernatural problem. The Kriminal Investigation Bureau was the public face as they pretended to be a law enforcement agency.

The Danish branch of the multinational organisation was new. So new, in fact, that it didn't yet have any operatives so Kretchmann and Kiel had been sent over the border from Germany to follow up on the latest report.

It had taken their government many decades to acknowledge the existence of supernatural creatures. Simple denial worked for most even though the evidence was there for them to see. Their boss, Bliebtreu claimed to have seen it first-hand; politicians' unwillingness to look facts in the face, always claiming what they were looking at, be it photographs, or video footage or eyewitness reports, could all be faked or simply misconstrued. All too often someone would point out that Hollywood could do even better with modern effects.

Finally though, when the son of the deputy Chancellor was killed by something they had no explanation for, he chose to chair a subcommittee that authorised the formation of a specialist unit which soon became the Supernatural Investigation Bureau, publicly known as the Kriminal Investigation Bureau and then renamed the Supernatural Investigation Alliance as they reached out to other countries to join them.

Now they spanned the globe though they struggled to recruit new members because they couldn't advertise what they were and had to do everything in secret.

Purpose was another thing they struggled with. Yes, there were supernatural creatures on the planet, but they were elusive and hidden, the Alliance usually finding out about them because there had been an attack. Everything they did was after the fact and they needed to get ahead of the game. However, each country operated in the manner they saw fit and though the Americans tried to lead everyone else, most countries ignored them.

The rise of reported incidents was growing exponentially, the boffin end of the Alliance always showing past trends to demonstrate that more and more people were vanishing because they were being snatched by something. Some bodies were found with strange marks on their necks. They now believed they knew what caused them, a supernatural creature which was almost impossible to catch because it could open a magical doorway and vanish through it. Dubbed vampires by the Alliance because they needed to call them something and they left a mark on their victim's necks, it used some kind of magical enchantment to disguise itself to look human. This made them even harder to find.

Recently they discovered the creatures were called Shilt. They were able to feed on the life energy of a person, essentially sucking the life out of their victims and now the boffins were trying to come up with a way to break through the enchantment – an anti-magic if you like, but so far they had nothing. What they needed was supernatural creatures to help them which was why they were chasing around trying to catch up to Zachary Barnabus. The Alliance held him captive previously, Barnabus electing to surrender to them in Leipzig. However, their previous boss, a man called Schmidt, had seen the shifter as a threat and locked him away deep underground intending to force him to cooperate. He escaped a week later with a wizard and they had been trying to relocate him ever since.

There were so many incidents for them to investigate, the Alliance could only cover twenty percent at any one time and they never really knew what they were chasing, or even if it was a real supernatural incident until they got there. Forced to prioritise which ones they sent men to, Bliebtreu, the boss in Germany, always went for those where the hope of capture was greatest.

They had two of the shilt in their facility in Berlin now, held way below ground where, for some reason, they were not able to open their magical gates. Schmidt had wanted information from the creatures they took captive and was quite happy to torture them if necessary. There was no law which could prevent him from doing so. That might have been tolerated if he had kept the practice to creatures like the shilt, but he was also kidnapping human citizens who possessed supernatural powers and holding them without process. When the wizard and the werewolf broke out, it exposed his illegal activities. Bliebtreu took over the next day so now they were looking for humans with supernatural abilities who might join the Alliance. Who better to help them in the quest against this menace but people who were themselves supernatural?

There was a tipping point coming, that was what the boffins said. All the countries in the Alliance calculated the same thing. They could trace supernatural visitations and incidents back more than two hundred years. They went further back than that but further back in time one looked, the more superstitious nonsense got mixed in with the truth. The point was that the increase in incidents could be measured and it was growing all the time like the population. Not only were they growing more prevalent, they were also spreading. The cases occurred in hubs, lots of them in a clustered area going back decades in most cases. Berlin was one such hub, but new hubs were appearing all the time. The problems in Bremen were a recent addition and just this week the first report came in from Munich. Coroners everywhere had been given photographs of wounds to look for and a number to call.

With the tracked growth, at some point, it would be constant and everywhere. Though no one could agree what that meant. There was a lot of conjecture about the Great Rapture, the end of times when God came to collect the chosen. Religious debate was inevitable, but Bliebtreu quashed it whenever he heard it; it wouldn't help them.

When they got wind of a man babbling about being attacked by a giant upright wolf in Denmark, Bliebtreu dispatched Kiel and Kretchmann. He wanted to go himself, but other matters were keeping him in Berlin.

Unfortunately, a day later, their investigation was already at a dead end; the trail going cold at the farm. It was him though; it was Barnabus, no doubt about it whatsoever. But just like every other time they followed up on a report, he had packed up and walked away, disappearing on foot in the middle of the night and the old couple weren't lying when they claimed they had no idea where he was going.

Kiel and Kretchmann talked about it a lot. They worked as partners, Bliebtreu insisting no one ever went out alone, so they spent a lot of time together. Both had joined the Alliance to make a difference and they were impatient. Impatient to demonstrate a result. They both felt they were losing the fight. The supernaturals, those who were not human, were coming to Earth from wherever was through their magical gateway and the SIA had no way to stop them.

There had been a few instances where local law enforcement had stumbled across a shilt feeding and challenged it. They lost in every case, usually getting killed themselves in the process but those who did survive would tell of their bullets being knocked from the air and the person they could see then vanishing through a circle of shimmering air - the magical gateway.

Given the chance, Kiel and Kretchmann would go through the gateway with an army and take the fight to them. Maybe this werewolf, only the fourth to be reported in the last decade, would be able to give them a vital clue, even if they had to cut it out of his brain. They liked to talk tough, both were ex-military, as were many of their colleagues; they posed as police officers and had some limited powers and training but the quest to bring in supernatural creatures wasn't for the faint-hearted. Secretly, they preferred Schmidt's methods, he didn't care what the politicians thought, he attacked the supernatural problem head on and would do whatever he thought was necessary. That was how Barnabus came to be locked up the first time. Bliebtreu was too softly-softly in their opinion; he wanted to coax the human supernaturals to help them in the fight.

Whatever the case, with the trail cold here, there was nothing they could do except return to Berlin. Bleibtreu had already instructed them to do so; he had other cases for them to explore. Barnabus's picture would be circulated and they would monitor police reports across Europe. He would turn up again somewhere and maybe next time they would get there before he moved on.

Maybe next time they would get to capture him.

Chapter 15

Z achary was three kilometres away before he started to calm down. He didn't blame Gitta for not believing him, he was confused by it too. The Kochs possessed magical ability which he bore witness to last night. It was different from Otto's; not as powerful for a start, and the tattoos made it look as if the magic was channelling through them, as if the Kochs had no ability of their own but had achieved it through the tattoos. If that was the case, he needed to find the tattoo parlour they used and shut it down. Their ability to use the magic for fighting hadn't impressed him, but the healing side of things was a problem. It was linked to their tattoos for sure but how that worked he had no idea.

Stopping to lean against a tree and think, he cursed himself for not leaving the diner straight away. He should have gone out to the front and proved he wasn't with them by beating all five into the dirt of the carpark. They might have chosen to reveal their magic at that point. He didn't know if the villagers already knew about it though he doubted they did, but reveal it or not, he couldn't see how they would be more effective than they had been last night.

Too late now, they hadn't hung around and he had dithered as he tried to work out what he could say to convince Gitta he wasn't the heel she now thought he was. He wouldn't have cared under different circumstances, he would just have moved on, but he knew she was in trouble. The whole village was, and he planned to save them all whether they asked him to or not.

Recognising that he should probably consider it to be a character flaw, he knew he wouldn't be able to sleep until he wiped the smile from Horst's face. Horst and Hans and any of the other Kochs who dared to defy him.

It would take a while to get to their house, he got directions from a gaggle of farmworkers outside the diner, but he had nowhere else he needed to be and nothing else he needed to do. It started to rain, fine, misty specks of it that blew about on the breeze barely heavy enough to be affected by gravity, but they damped his shirt until it stuck to him and then the fine drops became a steady drizzle.

It didn't bother him. If anything, it would help because the rain created a blanket of sound that would cancel out any noise he made when approaching their farm.

The walk took slightly more than an hour, moving in slow as he got nearer and keeping to the treeline so he wouldn't be seen. He wouldn't normally go to such lengths to remain undetected; he was more of a walk-up-and-kick-the-door kind of guy, but he wanted to know more about them before he attacked and that required some stealth and possibly even finesse; something he wasn't very good at.

Nevertheless, he came up on the Kochs' farmstead, found a spot in the treeline that allowed him to observe, and settled in. He needed to know more about their operation before he attempted to do anything. He needed to know if they had wives and children. If there were little ones at the house, or an elderly mother or some other potential innocent, he would have to pick a different place to confront them. Idly he fantasised about taking Horst's head back to Gitta and asking her if she still thought he worked for them while holding it in one hand.

Moments after settling in to watch the house, he saw four of the brothers, all of them except Peter, the youngest, get into their pickup trucks and leave. He settled in to wait for their return.

At some point, he fell asleep and the rain stopped, quiet countryside noises returning by the time he woke up. It was the sound of the vehicles bouncing back along the dirt track to the farm buildings that dragged him back to reality, but it was already beginning to get dark which had to mean it was getting close to six o'clock.

Zachary yawned and did his best to stretch in place without making himself visible. An apple from his backpack, which he snagged from a bowl in the kitchen before he left, was all he had but it would do for now. His stomach rumbled its emptiness, but it would be show time soon.

Full dark happened about an hour later. The Kochs had gone into their house and stayed there. Zachary thought it odd that five grown men, all brothers would live together still but it was a big house, easily big enough to accommodate all of them and families though there was no sign of anyone else here.

In several hours of observation, he had seen no children and no sign of anyone else here at all. There was no swing set or children's colourful slide in the grounds outside the house. No tiny bicycle with stabilisers and no feminine touches that might make him think there was a woman or women living with the men.

He was as certain as he could be without exploring the house. It was time to move in.

Zachary already knew what he was going to do and had made peace with the decision. The Kochs were a problem for the local population and the way they swung their weight around made him angry. They were the wolves and the villagers were the sheep and Horst made sure he reminded the sheep about their status regularly. Zachary was going to kill them. It would be easy enough and though he didn't want to be a killer, he doubted he would lose much sleep thinking about it.

He was a drifter, a nobody with no fixed abode, but he had a criminal record and the police would show up to a house with five bodies in it and be able to link him to the crime. However, if he shifted before he went in, the fingerprints and DNA he left wouldn't be those of Zachary Barnabus so the murders would never be tied to him. He wanted to know more about the Kochs, to learn more about their magical ability and where it came from but there was no time or opportunity for that. He was hardly going to befriend them now.

Stripped and transformed, he left his clothes in his backpack and stepped out of the treeline. Just as he did that, the front door opened, a shaft of light from inside creating a block of light in the darkness. A shadow filled it just before Rolf emerged. Hans was next, then Peter and then Manfred. Finally, Horst left the house, following behind the others as if herding them.

They walked single file and in silence as they crossed a dark yard area to a barn. They were invisible once they stepped into the black shadow cast by the barn or would have been if Zachary's werewolf vision wasn't so keenly able to see in the dark.

A light blinked twice inside the barn and then stayed on, the door closing once Horst was inside.

They were all in one place and away from the house, so any doubts he held about going in and finding there were elderly parents or anyone else inside evaporated. He was going into that barn and he would be the only one coming back out of it.

Chapter 16

Z achary kept up with the policy of invisibility, keeping to the shadows as he came near to the house, sidling around the buildings until he could cross to the barn without stepping into the moonlight. It was a cloudy night, the rain might have stopped but the sky threatened more, and it meant the natural light was minimal and he would be hard to see even if he did expose himself.

At the edge of the barn, he paused to listen, then spied light coming out from a gap between the boards. Peering inside, he could see the five men arranged in a half circle. Their bodies were bare from the waist up again and he could see the tattoos on their bodies glowing just as he had last night.

A voice came from inside. 'I'm telling you, Horst, we should have made sure.' Zachary moved about to see if he could get a better look at who was speaking, He thought it was Hans but couldn't be sure.

Horst's voice replied, 'And I told you we have no reason for concern.'

'He beat us easily, Horst. We were no match for him.' This time it was Rolf speaking.

'No match?' scoffed Horst. 'We are invincible. We cannot be killed. The runes Rebecca carved into our bodies ensures that.'

Who is Rebecca? The question swam to the surface of Zachary's consciousness even as he listened.

'She never said we couldn't be killed, Horst,' Hans pointed out.

'And yet we cannot. Last night was testimony to that. We healed in a few hours. Tonight, she will imbue us with enough power to defeat him if he ever shows his face again. In the meantime, we have weapons enough to defeat him.'

'You're guessing,' argued Rolf, directly challenging his eldest brother. Instantly there was a flurry of movement and the sound of a scuffle. Grunts and gasps as at least two of the men inside fought.

Peering through the gap, Zachary could see enough to know that Horst had put Rolf on his butt. 'Don't question me, Rolf,' raged Horst, standing over his brother. 'I'll not have it. I will guide this family to success. All that you have is by the grace of my hand. I brought Rebecca to us. I made us stronger than we could ever hope to be.'

Rolf wasn't done arguing, 'We don't even know what she is or why she is helping us, Horst.' His voice came out meek now though, shame at being beaten tailoring his attitude.

If Horst had a response to that, Zachary didn't hear it. Instead he heard Horst say, 'Prepare. She will join us soon. We must practice.'

Zachary found that he was itching to get inside and do what he came here for, but he was still arguing with himself about killing the five men. Since the incident at breakfast, when he could happily have bathed in their blood, his ire had cooled. Now it felt like a business decision and there was nothing to stop him walking away except his own sense of right and wrong.

The internal debate went on for more than a minute as, inside the barn, the five men conjured fire into their hands and pushed it outwards or conjured air, which Zachary could only see because it disturbed the dust as they threw it around.

Unable to reach a decision one way or the other, he went with his gut, shoving off the side of the barn with his shoulder. 'Screw it.'

'Did you hear something?' asked Peter, causing all the brothers to pause.

Then the barn door flew outwards as the angry werewolf gripped the handle and flung it open. As all heads turned his way, he paused in the doorway to say, 'Ding, ding. Round two.'

Then he was on them, not holding back this time as he charged into the room with his claws slashing. Peter fell backward in fright, which saved his life from a five-claw swipe. Zachary's hand passed through the space where his head had been half a second before, but momentum carried the werewolf onwards into the centre of the barn where the other brothers were all reeling.

The brothers were caught by surprise, but only momentarily. Flame and air leapt into their hands as together, the four of them attempted to push the enraged beast back. Zachary almost laughed that they would try the same tactics that proved so ineffectual last night, but the sound of a safety catch drew his eye to the right, where Horst was raising a handgun.

To Zachary's werewolf senses, it played out in slow motion. From the corner of his eye he could see Hans was also reaching behind his back as Manfred and Rolf tried to keep him at bay. They were capable of learning, opting to arm themselves with something that might do more damage their than insignificant magic tricks.

He was tough and he was fast, and he healed quickly, but he wasn't bullet proof. Gitta had asked him about it rhetorically just a few hours ago. If either man could get a shot off, he might be in trouble. Bullets would penetrate his skin, he knew that from painful experience, and though he would recover quickly enough, he had to admit some concern for what a bullet to his head might do. Immortality was a theory he didn't want anyone to test.

He didn't have enough time to alter the angle of his arm or change his stance enough to tag Horst with his claws, but he could swat at him with a fast backhand. His catcher's mitt sized left hand struck Horst on his right wrist, jarring the gun loose to send it flying across the room. All his inertia was going in an anticlockwise direction, a glance over his left shoulder assuring him there was no time to reverse direction before Hans, on his other side, got a shot off.

Using his left foot as a pendulum, Zachary overcame the problem by continuing the circle, spinning around despite the efforts of the brothers still wielding magic, until his right arm came back around.

Hans fired, pulling the trigger as an impulse reaction while still raising it to level. The bullet kicked up some dust and dirt close to Zachary's right foot, just before his rotation brought him all the way around.

With a snarl, Zachary whipped his right arm down, the hand moving at incredible speed on the outer edge of the circle he prescribed until it caught Hans in the middle of his right forearm and cut straight through it.

Another shot rang out as his muscles spasmed, but the gun, the hand, and part of his arm spun through the air over Rolf's head, the younger man unable to stop himself from watching it.

Zachary saw his distraction and kicked out with a thick leg, catching Rolf in his chest to punt him backward into the wall of the barn. It was over already, not even twenty seconds had elapsed, but Hans was out for good, Horst was disarmed, and Peter had most likely fled.

It was only then that a small voice inside his head reminded him about checking his six o'clock position.

The shot caught him high on his left shoulder blade. It had enough force to spin his body around as the pain from it crashed through his brain. Horst's gun. It had sailed across the room to fetch up at Peter's feet. As Zachary stumbled, tried to right himself and looked back toward the door, he saw the youngest man looking over the barrel, a classic two-handed pose and the close quarters giving him an easy shot.

Hans continued to scream about his hand, but Horst was ignoring him. He had a smile on his face, and he was moving to collect the weapon from Peter. He said, 'Well done,' as he raised his hand to beckon for the gun. He planned to finish Zachary off himself. Zachary wasn't that badly injured though. The bullet caught him by surprise but the moment the gun was handed over, he was going to strike, killing Horst and then Peter before finishing off the whole rotten crew.

He didn't get the chance.

Just as his muscles bunched in readiness to leap, a whisper on the air, 'Incensus,' made all five brothers drop to the floor. His eyes widened in surprise, and Zachary looked about to check they were all in the same state. None of them were moving save for their chests rising and falling with their breathing. Their eyes were open which made them look like they were awake, then movement made him whip around to face a darkened corner of the barn where a beautiful woman with flowing flame-red hair was now watching him.

Chapter 17

'Okay, now I'm lost.' Zachary threw his hands in the air and let them fall to his sides defeated. 'You must be Rebecca,' he said, making an educated guess from the overheard conversation earlier.

The woman had a curious smile. She hadn't spoken yet, other than the whispered word which dropped the Kochs and she appeared to be examining him, her eyes roving over his body, continuously moving until they returned to his face.

Her looks were quite startling; high cheekbones below piercing blue eyes which were so vibrant they looked to be glowing from within. Her figure was like something from the cover of a glossy fashion magazine. Her height was average at around one metre seventy though her slenderness made her seem taller. Her dress was black lace and either satin or silk; he never could tell the difference, but it clung to her body, showing every curve.

She took a step forward, her right foot appearing from beneath her dress to show bare skin. 'You know my name, but I do not know yours,' she cooed, her voice filled with flirtatious undertones which were echoed in her eyes.

As his libido reacted automatically to her attractiveness, he recognised how easily she had disarmed him, and fell back mentally into a defensive posture. 'Who are you? No, hold on,' he tutted and corrected himself. 'I know that one already. You're Rebecca and you like to handle more than one Koch at a time.' He studied her face to see how she would react to the insult but she either didn't understand it or just didn't care.

She continued to approach, her eyes roving his body again. 'You are hurt,' she announced, though there was no way she could see the wound on his shoulder.

His natural cockiness demanded a clever retort. 'It's just a scratch, babe.' It wasn't a scratch, it was a bullet wound and it hurt, his supernatural side notwithstanding. It was already healing but the bullet hadn't come out and he had to question whether that was a problem.

The woman moved gracefully as she stepped slowly around him, never getting too close until she came level with his shoulder and could see the wound for herself. 'I hardly think so,' she said, moving in to look at it. 'The projectile is still inside you. You have remarkable healing powers. How is that possible?' She was walking around him and asking questions as if they were having a conversation in a bar. Whoever she was, it was clear she held no fear. Had she seen a werewolf before? Did she possess an even higher level of magic than the Kochs? Eavesdropping their conversation led him to believe their magic came from her; that she had somehow imbued them with it so it made sense that she would be stronger.

He could observe her without moving his body, turning his head to the side allowed him to see that she was examining his back, so he saw when she brought her hands up and green light began to emanate from her palms.

'Whoa!' he turned around.

'I will heal you,' she offered. 'It is a simple spell.'

'You are a demon, yes?'

Rebecca's face registered surprise. 'A silly name given to us by your race, but yes, I am a demon. How do you know about us?'

He was dealing with another demon. She was smoking hot, but if she was anything like Teague then she was batshit crazy, deadly, and immortal. He had no argument with her though, provided she wasn't going to obstruct him dealing with the Kochs.

He chose to ignore her question, asking one of his own instead. 'Will you then heal them?' he asked, indicating the inert forms on the dirt floor. 'I came here to kill them. Fixing them up would spoil my plans.'

'Why do you wish to kill them?' she asked. 'They are my loyal servants.' Then she drew her hands apart to show they were empty but for the green light which hovered above them waiting for her to use it. 'Let me heal you and then we can discuss it.'

He didn't want to take a step back, he knew it would look weak, so as she advanced, he held up a hand to ward her off. 'I don't entirely trust you, lady. I know what demons are like and something you have done has turned these men into your personal sock puppets. I don't intend to suffer the same fate.'

'Sock puppet?' she repeated, failing to understand the reference. 'You are referring to their binding? They gave themselves to me willingly, I can assure you. They are my familiars. I have helped them, but they are weak. Not like you. Perhaps you would make a far superior familiar.'

He narrowed his eyes at her. 'You mean like a pet?'

'Oh, no, no, no. More like a servant. It brings me status. I hoped to elevate the tiny portion of magical energy these men were able to harness and make something useable from them. My blood gives them strength among other characteristics, and I have used ancient earth magic to enhance their meagre skills. However, I fear I may never be able to make them worthwhile.'

'You hear that, Kochs,' he bent his head down to look at Horst when he said it, getting his face close to the ground so the unmoving eyes might see him. 'Meagre. That's what the lady said about your skills.'

Rebecca continued to talk. 'I was considering moving on to look for a better specimen and here you are.' She smiled with pleasure as if she were offering him something he should rejoice in.

'I think I'll pass, lady,' Zachary said, shaking his head. More than ever, Zachary wanted to finish the job and move on. He could fight Rebecca, but experience had taught him that he couldn't kill a demon no matter what he did. That didn't mean he couldn't give as good as he got and maybe that would be enough to dissuade her from sticking around to cause trouble. Whether he could or couldn't, he wasn't going to be anyone's familiar.

Her smile faded into a look of disappointment, a frown settling over her delicate features. 'You are rejecting me?'

'Yeah, 'fraid so. You've got all kinds of crazy radiating off you.' He knew it was the wrong thing to say before he said it, he just didn't have the sense to hold his insult in.

Her frown turned to anger as she took a step forward and a sneer creased her mouth. 'You dare to insult me, mortal? I can kill you in an instant.' She pushed the green light still floating ethereally above her hands toward Hans and murmured another word Zachary heard but didn't understand, 'Incantus.'

Like a switch being thrown, the Kochs came back to life, four of them getting up while Hans managed to roll onto his feet. He held the stump of his right arm as the green light played over it. Zachary wondered for a moment if the missing limb was about to grow back but the spell appeared to be healing over the stump. Looking down at Hans as he quickly weighed up his options, he saw the man's eyes when they snapped in his direction, filled with hate and the need for vengeance.

Now what? Did he put them down again? Would Rebecca try to stop him? He was completely surrounded and standing in the middle of a circle as they hemmed in on every side.

'Now you die,' snarled Horst though he kept his distance from the deadly claws and wasn't trying to conjure a spell of any kind.

Rebecca said, 'No.' her tone insistent and clearly expecting no argument. Then she brought her hands together, light sparking down her arms both over and under her skin as it made its way to her hands. The passage took less than a second and she drew her hands apart with a white chord of energy between them which she flicked at Zachary, letting go with her left hand and holding it with her right. It wrapped around him like a magical lasso, yanking his arms in tight to his sides, then she moved her left hand, controlling the spell as she lifted him off his feet. 'You will surrender to my will, shapeshifter. How soon you chose to do so will dictate how much you suffer.'

Then she did something which sent a wave of energy into him along the glowing white thread of the lasso. It tore into his body, like electrical worms burrowing into his nerves. It felt like being set on fire from the inside and there was no escape.

The Kochs leered and smiled, especially Hans who moved around to make sure he could look into Zachary's face. The last thing Zachary saw before he passed out was Peter skulking at the back and looking like he wanted to be anywhere else.

Chapter 18

Boris Mailer took the job in SIA, The Supernatural Investigation Alliance, six weeks ago and had regretted it ever since. He had fervently believed in everything supernatural ever since he was big enough to understand the concept. Growing up on his older brother's comic books and old black and white Hammer horror movies, he wanted to be like Peter Cushing and slay the evil creatures. Of course there were no real supernatural monsters for him to battle so he joined the police and lived what he felt to be a humdrum life until a random test he didn't even remember taking made him a suitable candidate to apply for a division of the police he had never even heard of.

The invitation to apply came in a real envelope, not an email from Human Resources, which struck him as odd, but the letter contained no information about the division other than that he was deemed to be a suitable candidate and if he wanted to apply he needed to report to the office of the Kriminal Investigation Bureau on Kitzner Strasse in Berlin on Monday, January 12th.

He asked people at the station, but no one had ever heard of the division and he could find no reference to it even on the internet. It was bizarre enough to make him want to know more, so he took a day off, caught the train and travelled from Bielefeld to Berlin, took a taxi to Kitzner Strasse, and found the office in a nondescript office block.

It wasn't the office for a police division though, he knew that the moment he walked in. Walking out ninety minutes later after signing a host of confidentiality agreements, he could barely feel the earth beneath his feet. The supernatural did exist! Not only that, he was joining a team to hunt and capture the creatures he read about as a boy.

Six weeks later, with an empty bank account from moving to a new city and zero life because his girlfriend dumped him, he was yet to leave the office and was getting quite despondent. He wasn't cleared for field operations yet so all he could do was office work and nod obediently to the bosses.

When the phone rang, it startled him and interrupted a game of solitaire he was playing on the computer. 'Kriminal Investigation Bureau, Detective Mailer.'

Ten minutes later, he knocked on the closed office door of Deputy Commissioner Bliebtreu, a neat man with a crew cut and a hard stare. When called to enter, he checked his clothing to make sure he looked neat and went inside to deliver the news: Zachary Barnabus had caught a lift from a long-distance driver. It happened two days ago, and the man had dropped him off in Bad Dorstel.

Chapter 19

A gentle caress to his left cheek woke him, his eyes fluttering open to find Rebecca crouched in front of his face. She smiled down at him, a pleasant smile like a mother might show to her child. 'How are you feeling, Zachary?'

He levered himself off the ground with one elbow, propping himself upright so he was looking at her face to face. He was no longer a werewolf, his body transforming back to its human state when he lost consciousness. He also wasn't bound, but as he realised that and lunged for her, she hit him with the lasso thing again. The burst of pain was brief this time, intended only to get his attention.

Annoyed at his behaviour, she snapped, 'This is unproductive, Zachary. I am offering you my help.'

'By torturing me.'

'No. That is just a side effect of your unrelenting stubbornness. I have already removed the bullet from your back. You feel no pain or discomfort there anymore, do you?' He rolled his shoulder experimentally. She was right; he felt not even the slightest stiffness where the bullet had entered. 'You see? We can be friends, Zachary. All you need to do to escape the suffering you will otherwise endure, is to submit to me. Agree to be my student.'

'You mean slave,' he growled, trying to prepare himself for the next wave of agony.

'Slave is such an ugly word,' she replied snippily. 'Do the brothers act as if they are unhappy with our relationship? I have made them far stronger than they were; than they ever could have been. Now I want to do the same for you and all I need is a drop of blood.'

He struggled against the bond, the veins standing out all over his body as he bucked and thrashed, but mere muscle wasn't going to break the spell holding him in place. Through gritted teeth, he snarled, 'I think you should get on the torture part again, lady, the sound of your voice is boring me.'

White hot pain lanced through his body instantly, tearing into his soul it seemed as the blackness took him once more.

The next time external noises and sensations invaded his consciousness, he heard the Kochs talking. The unmistakable voice of Horst grumbling somewhere behind him. He was awake but his eyes were closed as he remained still and listened quietly.

He heard Rolf speak, 'We can't kill him, Hans. She wants him alive.'

Hans argued. 'I don't care what she wants. He took my hand, so I'm going to cut his head off.'

'What then, Hans?' Rolf sounded exasperated, like the discussion had been going on for a long time now. 'What? We say he was escaping, and it was an accident?'

'Tell her what you like, Rolf. I don't care. Look at me! Look at my arm!' Short, snappy footfalls preceded a hard kick to his kidney which Zachary had to fight hard not to react to. The blow gave him the chance to move, which he hadn't dared do yet. He wanted to know if he was tied up and he got his answer. The motion of the kick was enough to rattle the chains tied around him. He was handcuffed ankles and wrists with a thick chain going between the two. Even transformed it would be difficult, if not impossible, to break out of them. Getting enough leverage would be the problem.

A scuffle broke out behind him and though he couldn't see what was happening, he got the gist which was that Hans wanted to kick him to death and Rolf was holding him back.

Horst, who had remained quiet for a while, intervened. 'Enough. Rebecca said she wants him held until she can return so that is what we will do. We have plenty of other tasks we can attend to.'

'Such as?' grumbled Hans, very much disgruntled.

'Such as dealing with the diner. I am fed up being polite. I think we should just make Gitta and her mother disappear.' He waited for comment, probably looking around the room to see if his brothers would challenge him.

It was Peter who spoke out. 'I don't want to hurt them. She has a little girl.' His voice was too meek when he said the words. It told everyone listening that he already knew he was going to be ignored so they should go right on and do it.

Hans laughed at him. 'Still hoping to get into her pants, Peter? She's never shown you the slightest interest.'

The comment struck a nerve somewhere deep inside, Peter screaming with frustration as he ran at his brother to bowl him over. With only one arm, Hans was finally on the receiving end but as the youngest brother grabbed two fistfuls of hair to slam Hans's head into the ground, Rolf hauled him off.

'I'll kill you too!' screamed Hans, apoplectic with rage. 'You and the werewolf and that bitch at the diner and Rebecca if she wants to stop me.

Ever the voice of calm, Horst said, 'I think that's enough for now. Rolf, are you sure his cuffs are secure?'

Rolf huffed out a breath and came over to check them, rattling both wrist and ankle cuffs and then checking the chain in between that would prevent Zachary from standing upright even if he could get to his feet. 'Hey, I think he's awake.'

Zachary exploded into motion, whipping out with both hands to club the smaller man in the face with both fists and the cuffs together. Then he followed him as Rolf recoiled from the blow, rolling on top of him to get the chain around his neck. He almost made it too.

Horst got to his hands, just as Manfred grabbed his feet. Zachary bucked and thrashed again but even with his strength he couldn't overcome being pulled in three directions at once.

Once they got him away from Rolf, they all stood back, a single line of brothers all staring down at him lying naked on the floor.

'Where's Rebecca?' he growled, his deep rumbling bass carrying threat and menace even though chained.

'That's not for you to be concerned about,' replied Horst. 'She'll return soon enough. In the meantime. You just stay comfortable in here. I know it's cold, but I think a tough guy like you can handle it.'

Zachary looked at Hans, making sure he had eye contact before he asked, 'If you're going to leave me here, could you give me a *hand* up?'

Hans's eyes widened as rage took him and it was all Rolf and Manfred could do to hold him back.

'Wow,' said Zachary with a chuckle. 'That was quite something. I thought you were going to get the upper *hand* then. I think that was a valiant effort. Everyone, let's have a show of *hands* if you agree.'

Hans screamed bloody murder in reply, spitting and cussing as his brothers held him back.

Horst said, 'One more hand joke and I'll tell them to let him go.'

Zachary nodded his understanding. 'Thank you for the warning, Horst. I wouldn't want to overplay my *hand*.'

Hans bellowed as he broke free, Rolf and Manfred doing nothing to stop him as he charged. It was exactly what Zachary wanted, Hans receiving a devastating head butt as Zachary thrust the whole top half of his body forward. Hans bounced off, his face exploding with a spray of blood. Zachary could have followed him down and done more damage, but he knew the brothers would instantly be on him and their combined effort would be enough to haul him off.

Instead, he turned his gaze toward Horst. 'I'll leave him in your safe *hands*, shall I?'

Angry, Horst snapped at his younger brothers. 'Get Hans up and get him back to the house.' His eyes never left Zachary's as they hauled up their barely conscious brother. 'The only reason you are still alive is because Rebecca wants you that way. She intends to break you herself, but I will have my revenge, pretty boy. You can bank on that.'

Horst lingered as the others left but once they were outside, he followed them and shut the door. Through the doorway, Zachary could see the sun was coming up. The sky was still dark, but the first tendrils of dawn were beginning to penetrate the gloom. The entire night had gone by while he was either out cold or being driven mad by Rebecca's torture methods.

For the next hour, he hopped about the barn trying to find something he could use as a key to get the cuffs off; an old nail, a forgotten tool, anything that he might get into the keyhole and be able to use. Alternatively, was there something he could use to break the chain? He was all kinds of strong and just needed something he could use as a lever, but both searches prove fruitless.

He shifted, taking his werewolf form, but that too failed to give him the freedom he needed. He couldn't get out of the barn and hop away either because they were bright enough, or, worryingly, well-practiced enough, to have secured his chain to a large ring sunk into concrete in the ground. He tried to force that out, grunting and straining against it but he needed leverage and had none.

Dawn broke outside, he could see the light coming through dozens of tiny gaps in the wood. It frustrated him, he could feel the ticking clock reminding him with each second that Horst was going to do something to Gitta today and he needed to escape but couldn't. That Rebecca would return for round two later, presumably when it got dark again, was of limited concern. She could waste as much time as she liked torturing him. He wouldn't submit no matter what she did, and she couldn't kill him just as he couldn't kill her.

For now, though, there was nothing he could do.

He settled onto the ground to wait

Chapter 20

Two hundred and fifty kilometres away, Deputy Commissioner Bliebtreu was on the phone to a truck driver called Hermann Shultz, confirming when and where he dropped off Zachary Barnabus. That he had indeed carried the man they sought was no longer in question so far as Bliebtreu was concerned. The only questions he had were how fast they could get to Bad Dorstel and whether Barnabus would still be there when they arrived.

Bliebtreu had agents operating all over Europe, the Alliance had quickly become a borderless, multi-lingual operation and Germany was one of the largest hubs because they were one of the first to create a division to address the growing problem. Only the Americans and oddly the Guatemalans had beaten them to it.

He wanted to send a sizeable force after Barnabus, not to capture him but to show him that they could but wouldn't. He wanted Barnabus to work for them, they would benefit immensely from having supernaturals in their ranks. Unfortunately, he just didn't have the manpower to do that right now, so his strategy was to send a small team. They could scope out the situation without attracting the attention a large force would, and report back. If Barnabus was there, he would go himself.

Mailer was still waiting patiently to be dismissed or given an order. He was starting to feel uncomfortable as if he had been forgotten and the right thing to do was just leave, but he had already been standing there for so long it seemed awkward to move now.

Bliebtreu chose that moment to look up. 'Mailer, well done for this.' Mailer nodded at being acknowledged though all he had done was answer the phone. 'Get Kiel and Kretchmann up here, fast as you can.'

His feet started moving, but at the door he asked, 'What's going on, sir?' Hoping for something of interest to take his mind off the boredom.

'Are you cleared for field ops yet?'

Huffing out a breath of disappointment, Mailer said, 'No, sir.'

Bliebtreu wriggled his lips from side to side as he stared into space. He looked like he was trying to decide something. When he looked back up, he said, 'Well, now you are. Get Kiel and Kretchmann, you are going with them.' Bliebtreu knew he wasn't supposed to send agents into the field until they had been through a full training package. They needed to know what they were dealing with and how to stay alive, but they were just going to observe. Mailer could do the training later.

Mailer ran back to his office bursting with excitement. Bliebtreu could have called the two men to his office using his phone, but why hire a dog if you are going to bark yourself? Quickly shutting down his computer, Mailer then jogged down to where he expected to find Kiel and Kretchmann. They were back from their last op and hadn't gone out again yet, so he found them in the shooting range, where many of the former armed forces operatives hung out. Mailer was one of the few that migrated into SIA from the police force and found himself the butt of constant jokes.

'Hey, it's the rookie,' announced Kiel the second Mailer came into the room. Kretchmann looked up from cleaning his weapon but didn't bother to speak. He was sitting at a small table with the weapon laid out in pieces. Kiel was sitting on the table with one foot dangling and the other on the seat of a chair.

Mailer bit his lip at the unnecessary comment and delivered his news. 'I think I have found Barnabus. Bliebtreu wants the three of us to confirm his location and report back.'

'Kiel raised an eyebrow. 'You're coming with us? I thought you were a desk jockey.'

'I got cleared for field work.'

Kretchmann slammed the last part of his weapon back into place with the flat of his hand, checked the action was smooth and stood up. 'Let's go, Kiel. I'm bored here.'

Kiel got to his feet as well, sliding off the table to head for the door. Over his shoulder he said, 'Go and check out a weapon from the armoury. In fact, check out a couple and make sure you have plenty of ammunition.'

'Bliebtreu just wants us to observe,' Mailer pointed out.

Kiel turned around to walk backward as he got to the door. With a smile, he said, 'And that's what we are going to do, desk jockey. But out there, things don't always go according to plan, so let's take some protection with us just in case, okay?'

As Mailer dashed away, Kretchmann tapped his colleague on the arm, 'We're going to bring him in, right? Not this observe crap Bliebtreu wants.'

Kiel nodded; they were both bored with the lack of action. They hadn't fired a gun outside of a range since they joined the SIA. 'It won't be difficult to come up with a reason why we needed to move in. He was about to hurt someone, we thought there was danger to the civilian population. We can say anything we like because it'll be pats on the back all around when we bring him in.'

'You think Mailer will be a problem?'

'Maybe. We can scope out his politics in the car and if we have to *accidentally* ditch him somewhere so we can move freely, then so be it.'

Chapter 21

M ore than an hour after they left him in the barn, Zachary heard one of the pickup trucks start up. It had to be almost twenty-four hours now since he left the diner and he was willing to bet the pickup that just left was heading there right now.

A minute of angrily shaking the chains and yanking at them succeeded only in bruising his wrists and cutting into the flesh. He couldn't see who had gone out in the pickup, but he was sure only one had gone, not both, so it stood to reason that not all the Kochs had departed. He further surmised that it would be Hans left behind since he was suddenly missing a hand plus one of the brothers. Which one he couldn't tell. Horst wouldn't want to take Peter, especially if they were going to the diner to do something about Gitta and her mother. Equally, he wouldn't want to leave him behind to keep Hans in check.

Either way, he wasn't surprised when he heard footsteps on the gravel outside and heard the lock on the barn door being opened. Whoever was out there dropped the padlock, cursing angrily as they yanked the latch on the door.

'Would you like a *hand* out there?' called Zachary, guessing correctly that it was Hans returning. And he couldn't hide the smirk on his face as the second eldest Koch ripped open the door with his left hand, his face an angry mask.

'You won't think it's funny soon,' Hans snarled, yanking the door to slam behind him. It smacked against the wood and sprang open again, not that Hans cared. He held up his stump. 'I can't even conjure magic now. Rebecca wants you alive and Horst insists I can't kill you. No one said anything about leaving you in one piece though.' With a triumphant smile, he pulled a long bowie knife from behind his back, waving it in the air as he held it clumsily in his left hand.

Zachary fixed his face, wiping the smirk off to present Hans with a serious expression. He needed it for his next question. 'Tell me, Hans, you're the shortest of your family, but is that the real reason the villagers all refer to you as tiny Koch?'

Hans rushed him, just as Zachary hoped he would, bellowing his rage as he charged with the knife leading. Zachary knew he was going to get stabbed; he couldn't see a way around it. The chains stopped him from standing upright so the best he could achieve was a bent-kneed crouch. Hans would run to him and try to stick him with the knife. Not that Zachary wanted a knife in him, but if it went that way, he would recover from the wound within minutes and he would know where the knife was, plus it would definitely place Hans within striking distance. If he could get him down, Hans was as good as dead. Then Zachary just had to hope Hans had the handcuff keys on him somewhere.

Hans had five metres of ground to cover, then four, then three as he picked up speed and Zachary readied himself, focussing on nothing but the approaching madman and the knife in his hand. If he timed it right, he might get away uninjured.

Two metres. Then Hans's forward motion ceased as a large black-skinned hand gripped around his neck. Hans's feet flew out from underneath him, their inertia unchecked, and then Hans flew sideways, whipping across the barn to crunch against a wall with a loud bang. One of the wooden panels broke as his head went partially through it. Zachary only caught that out of the corner of his eye though because he was focused on what was now standing where Hans had been.

Directly in front of him, clouds of vapour forming above its head as it breathed, was a werewolf.

It stood upright on legs just as he did and looked just as Zuzanna had in Bremen. It was smaller than Zuzanna, who had been almost as big as Zachary at close to two and a half metres tall, however it was still enormous and deadly looking.

Zachary's face broke into a broad grin. There was a werewolf here. He had found it, or, more accurately, it had found him. He also knew who it was.

He couldn't help but smile as he said, 'Hello, Gitta.' The werewolf tilted its head in question. 'I saw the dirt on your feet two nights ago. When I came back from going with the Kochs and you joined me a for a drink before bed, I saw it when you walked away. You had been outside and come back in but hadn't had time to clean them off. Or you had forgotten to. Whichever the case, I knew what it was because I have the same problem. Sometimes I have bits of undergrowth or brambles in my hair, but always the dirty feet.'

To fill in a blank, just in case one existed, he shifted as well, holding his breath as he went from one state to the other.

The werewolf standing opposite hadn't spoken yet, but when he changed form it darted back a metre in shock. 'Oh, my God!' it cried, the voice distinctly Gitta's but now with a husky edge which to his ears made her sound sexy, like it was her bedroom voice or something.

He transformed back to his human form, keen to get out of his chains if he could. Transforming in them had been painful as his wrists and ankles swelled to fill the internal diameter of the cuffs and the chain between them made sure he had to stay bent over. Conscious that he was naked, he pointed to Hans. 'Can you check if he has keys on him?'

Gitta the werewolf glanced at Hans and back at Zachary. 'Um, yeah sure.' Her mind was reeling from the revelation that he was a shifter. All these years she never thought she was the only one, but it never occurred to her to go looking for others. Her mother knew her secret, but no one else did and the shifter gene hadn't come from her mother because there was nothing remotely supernatural about her. Gitta's father was a drunken accident at a music festival in Dortmund when her mother was eighteen years old so maybe it came from him. Or maybe it wasn't genetic at all. She had hidden it all her life and hardly ever shifted. In fact, she hadn't changed form in the best part of a year and the last time she did, that idiot Gruber had seen her and called a reporter. She had been out trying to track some deer. The meat was free if she caught it herself and it would take off some of the pressure the Kochs were putting on them if they didn't have to buy meat. Since Gruber saw her, she hadn't changed once until two nights ago when she set out to see if she could find Zachary and stop the Kochs from killing him.

There was something in Hans' pocket but with her oversized werewolf hands she couldn't get into it.

Zachary saw her struggling. 'Just change into human form,' he suggested.

She narrowed her eyes at him. 'I'll be naked.'

He rolled his eyes and looked down at himself. 'I'm already naked.'

'All the more reason for me to not be.'

'Good grief, Gitta. It's not like I can do anything about it if you do get naked. I'm quite convincingly chained up and chained to the ground.'

It wasn't so much that Gitta was self-conscious about her body, she thought she looked good naked, but she didn't entirely trust herself to be naked around Zac; shifting form wasn't the only thing she hadn't done for more than a year.

Coming up with an alternative plan, she left the unconscious Hans on the dirty barn floor and stood up. 'I'm going to get some scissors,' she announced and ran out of the door.

'Wait,' Zac yelled but she was already gone. 'You can use a claw to cut his pocket open,' he called after her even though he knew she was out of earshot.

A chicken squawked its disapproval somewhere over toward the house as she went looking for scissors, but he wasn't waiting for her to return. He was sitting on his backside and couldn't stand upright in the chains, so he scooted/crab-walked across to see if he could reach Hans. The fallen Koch was just a little out of reach even with Zachary's long arms. Growling at the sky for all the inconveniences, he transformed again, which gave him the extra ten centimetres of reach he needed to snag the man's foot.

The keys were in his pocket, but Zachary had to shift back to human, getting his hands on them just as Hans came around again to find a naked man fiddling around near his groin.

'What the?' Hans asked, his eyes darted down to where Zachary's hand was rooting around and back up to Zachary's face.

'Don't worry,' Zachary assured him just before he punched him with his free hand. Hans's eyes rolled back in his head once more as Zachary pulled the keys free. 'You're not my type.'

When Gitta came back in half a minute later, Zachary was free of the chains and stretching as tall as he could go to ease off his back. Being scrunched up for so many hours was tough, even if he was immortal and had impossibly fast healing powers.

'I found some... oh.' Gitta brandished the scissors but they were clearly not necessary. She looked around for somewhere to put them down, scanning about for a table or something before realising she was being ridiculous and tossing them in a corner. 'You, ah ... you got the keys then?'

'Yes. Thank you for coming for me by the way.' Zachary had hold of his head with both hands, the right on top of his skull and the left under his jaw as he twisted his head around to stretch off his neck. 'Can I assume you no longer believe I work for the Kochs?'

'No,' Gitta replied, saw Zachary's right eyebrow rise and corrected herself. 'I mean yes. Yes, you can assume that. No, I no longer think you work for them.'

'What caused the change of heart?' Zachary was done stretching but he had a headful of questions. Gitta was a shifter, that made them very compatible and he was already attracted to her. Not only that, in theory they were both naked. If she would just transform back into her human form, they could have all kinds of fun. Gitta just looked nervous though, all out of place and trying to work out where to look.

'Um, it was my mum actually. She pointed out that you didn't go with the Kochs when they left and when you left you didn't follow them. She also said you didn't have a phone so couldn't have been communicating with them. She searched your room when you left that first afternoon. Well, we both did, truth be told. Then, I heard that you asked for directions to their farm so you couldn't have known where it was ... sorry,' she said, looking away again. 'Can you please put something on?'

Zachary looked around. 'I don't have anything to put on. My clothes are out there somewhere. Or should be if the Kochs didn't find them.'

'Well, can you cover that... cover it up,' she begged. Gitta was finding Zachary's naked groin a little too distracting. It kept jiggling when he moved. He was clearly loving how uncomfortable his nakedness was making her, a big grin plastered across his face that she half wanted to slap, and half wanted to kiss.

'How about if I shift, will that make you more comfortable. It's less noticeable then.' He closed his eyes and shifted from human form to werewolf.

Gitta breathed a sigh of relief. 'Thank you. Now, where was I?'

'You were admitting that you are not very trusting and like to go through other people's things.'

'Hey,' she complained. 'You just showed up out of nowhere.'

He held up a hand of surrender as he chuckled, 'I'm just kidding, Gitta. You were telling me that your mum didn't trust me but, in the end, decided that I might be telling the truth. Did you know I was a werewolf?'

'God no. No, I had no idea until you changed form when I came in here. I've never met another shifter. Have you?'

'Only one,' he answered quietly. He didn't want to dwell on Zuzanna or give Gitta the chance to ask questions, so he changed the subject quickly. 'What did you do about Horst this morning?'

She tilted her head in question. 'What do you mean?'

'He left here a while back heading to the diner. I think he planned to get mean with you about the diner and his money. Did you know about their magic? Did you know they have enslaved themselves to a demon?'

Gitta had stopped listening though; her brain had just hit panic mode and she was backing toward the door. 'I left early this morning to look for you. They must have turned up while I was here and that means ... Paula.'

Chapter 22

Gitta ran out of the door with Zachary hard on her heels. It didn't sit well with him to leave Hans alive but there was no time to deal with him now, not if Paula was in trouble. Gitta was still in werewolf form and running for the road. Zachary's shout stopped her.

'The car is faster!' She had already run past it but turned to look at him. He held the keys in his hand; they were on the same bunch as the handcuff key he used to get free. He was right, the big Mercedes pickup truck would be faster. She ran back to him, heading for the passenger door but that's where he was, and he got in before she could say anything.

'What are you doing?' she asked.

'I can't drive,' he explained, looking apologetic. 'I left home at seventeen and never learned.'

She held up her huge, meaty werewolf hands. 'I can't drive like this.' He shrugged and held out the keys.

Cursing under her breath, she snatched the keys from his outstretched hand and stomped around to the driver's side of the car to get in. Then stood by the door for two seconds while she changed back into human form.

Zachary smiled at her and made no attempt to not look at everything she had to show him. 'You better stop grinning,' she growled a warning.

He laughed as he turned his face to look out of the windscreen. 'You ought to be glad I'm not drooling.'

The engine caught and there was no further need for conversation as she mashed the accelerator pedal to propel the car down the gravel driveway and out onto the highway. Getting back to the diner took only a few minutes, Gitta bursting from her door almost before the truck stopped moving. The back door was open, Gitta snagging a coat as she went through the small entrance lobby. Zachary took one as well, not that it would fit his shoulders, but he didn't want the little girl to see him naked, so he wrapped it around his waist and used the two arms to tie a knot so it stayed there.

Gitta was flustered, her heart pounding in her chest as she yelled for her mother and daughter. She already knew they were not here, but she had to keep looking, praying they were hiding somewhere, or maybe just tied up and gagged. She took her phone from the nightstand where she left it and dialled her mother's phone. A second later she heard it ringing in her mother's bedroom.

With panic rising, she ran from room to room, screaming Paula's name in a frantic bid to find her little girl. By the time Zachary's voice reached her thirty seconds after they came into the diner, she was already sobbing and vowing mentally to make the Kochs pay. It had occurred to her before that she had the ability to dispense with the Kochs. She was a werewolf and that made her both powerful and deadly. She wasn't a killer though. How could she sleep at night after murdering five men? It would have to be all of them too. If she killed Horst, Hans would take over and he would most likely be worse. Only Peter had a good bone in his body, but none of that mattered because she wasn't a killer.

Until now. Now they had taken her daughter. She knew it even without seeing any evidence and it was enough to make her want to shift form and then tear them apart.

'Gitta.' Zachary called her name again. His voice was soft, as if he had bad news to share with her and sombre was the correct timbre to use.

She found him in the bar where a handwritten note was pinned to the bar with a large hunting knife.

'They have her, don't they?' she asked quietly, advancing slowly toward the note. She needed to read it, but she desperately didn't want to.

Zachary nodded, taking a step to the side so she could get to the piece of paper. It was a hurried scrawl from Horst.

We have Meg and Paula. You can have them back and they will not be harmed but this nonsense with the diner has gone on too long. You will come to the old barracks tonight. You will bring the deeds to the diner or the little girl and your mother will suffer. If you call the police, you will never see them again. I will message you when I am ready for you to come.

A tear rolled down her face. She pulled her phone from the pocket she stuffed it into and scrolled until she found Horst's number. Waiting for it to connect seemed to take forever, but it gave her time to run through what she wanted to say in her head. She wanted to scream at him, to call him names and promise to rip out his spleen, but that wouldn't get her the result she wanted. She would agree to anything he said just to get her little girl back. Then, she would see about settling the score.

Horst didn't answer though. The phone just rang until the voicemail connected. She tried again. And then again and then sent him a text message telling him he could have whatever he wanted so long as he gave Paula back unharmed. She tried not to think about her tiny daughter with those men.

Zachary moved in behind her, putting his arms around her for comfort. It gave her something to cling to as she wept.

'We are going to get them,' he breathed into her ear. 'What they can do is no match for me, or for you.' Then he was quiet, and they just stayed that way for a while.

Chapter 23

The hug wasn't going anywhere, and it wasn't getting them anywhere. It was Zachary that broke it, unfolding his arms to let her go and stepping back. She turned around to face him, finding that he had a determined set to his mouth.

'Right now, they are holding all the cards. At least that's how they see it. We have to get them off balance, take the advantage away from them.'

'They said no cops,' she repeated Horst's words quietly.

He met her eyes. 'A policy I happen to agree on. I don't trust law enforcement at all; I mean to scupper their plans myself.'

'Hold on,' she remembered something he said earlier back in the barn. She heard it, but all she could think about at the time was her daughter and what Horst might do. Now it came back to her. 'You said something about them being able to do magic.'

He raised an eyebrow.

'Back at the barn. You said the Kochs have magical powers, or something like that and you said something about a demon. I wasn't really listening because you had just told me they were coming here.'

'Oh. When you didn't reply and didn't question me about it, I figured you already knew, and it was old news.'

'No, sorry. I just couldn't get my brain to process the information and I only just remembered it. They can do magic. Like dangerous stuff?'

Zachary opened his mouth, intending to belittle what they could do, but stopped himself. If Gitta was going to face them, she needed to know they might be able to hurt her. Just because they couldn't do much to him, didn't mean they couldn't injure her. 'What do you know about demons?' he asked.

She narrowed her eyes at him; this wasn't the time for messing around but while she picked up within hours of meeting him that he had a fast tongue and liked to joke, she got no sense now that he wasn't being serious. 'Demons?' she repeated. 'You're serious.'

He huffed a breath out through his nose wondering where to start. 'I want to start by admitting that I don't know what I am talking about.'

Gitta snorted out a little laugh. 'That's comforting.'

'Yeah.' He scratched his head. 'A little while ago, I met a wizard and we went through a portal conjured by a disgusting creature called a shilt to a realm where there are demons.'

Gitta was listening but couldn't help saying something, 'This sounds like the start of a bad joke.'

'Don't worry, it gets worse,' he assured her. 'I think that at some point in the past, the demons lived on earth with us. That's how it was explained to me. The demons, the shilt, lots of other magical creatures lived on earth with the humans and all the other non-magical creatures. Then something happened, the demons' supreme being was murdered by a jealous son and he cast a death curse that split them from Earth to trap them in a new realm – a new version of Earth where just the magical creatures would live. They were made immortal, so they had forever to think on their sins, but the death curse has weakened over the years and they are finding their way back.'

'How do you know all this?' she asked him, astounded by what she was hearing. 'How come no one else knows?'

'Well, *know* would be a misleading word to use. I wouldn't claim that I know anything, but the wizard, a guy called Otto, he's German by the way, he seemed to know what he was talking about and this was how he explained it to me. As for no one else knowing. I think the death curse failing and the demons coming to Earth is a recent thing. Certainly, someone knows about it because there is a group called the Supernatural Investigation Alliance; right bunch of dicks they are. They know about it. They approached me in a weak moment and conned me into going with them, then they locked me up. That's where I met the wizard.'

'But what does this have to do with the Kochs?'

'I'm getting there, honest.' He was trying to tell it in a way that made it less confusing, but he was doing a bad job if her face was anything to go by. 'The demons, some of them at least, want to capture humans who possess magical ability. They use them as familiars, which I think is just a nice word for slave. It gives them status apparently. I learned that bit last night while I was being tortured by Rebecca.'

'Who the hell is Rebecca?' Gitta was getting angry now. Not at Zachary, it wasn't his fault, but she thought she was going up against the Kochs and would gladly rip them apart if the opportunity presented itself. Now she had demons and magic to consider as well?

Zachary pressed on. 'Rebecca is a demon and she has taken the Kochs as her familiars. She's got a totally smoking hot body, but she is batshit cra ...' his sentence trailed off as he noticed her expression.

'Totally smoking hot?'

'Um. Well ... obviously I haven't seen her naked yet, so cannot do a full side by side comparison, but I'm willing to bet you would come out as the victor.

'You haven't seen her naked *yet*.' Gitta hit the yet bit hard, making sure he got the point.

He didn't say anything for a moment, sensing that he had snagged an invisible tripwire somewhere but unsure quite what her stern tone was supposed to tell him.

'I'm just going to move on with the story, I think.'

'Maybe you should,' she agreed, her eyes still pinched.

He went back over what he had been telling her in his head and picked up where he left off. 'So, she's probably a bit crazy, but she has taken the Kochs as her familiars. All five of them. She wears a brand like mark for each of them about here.' He indicated a point above his heart about halfway between his nipple and his clavicle. 'She has imbued them with magical ability. I think they each possessed a trace amount, but they have tattoos on them that are not really tattoos.' He saw her about to ask what they were if they weren't really tattoos and quickly added, 'They glow when they touch them. I think she has used some kind of ancient demon magic to enhance their natural level and then trained them. I caught them practicing their spell casting when I went to their farm last night.'

'What sort of spells,' asked Gitta.

It was a pertinent question. 'I think they call it elemental magic. It's what Otto can do, only he is vastly more powerful than them. When I fought them in the woods on Friday night, they only used air and fire. I don't think she has taught them how to do other spells yet, but it may just be that they didn't use them. Air can push you or knock you down. Fire can burn you, but it doesn't have much impact on my skin. If you are anything like me when transformed, then it will warm you nicely but that's about it. They got over their inability to hurt me last night by bringing guns to the party. They were ready for me, not that it did them much good.' he added quickly.

'How come I found you chained to the floor then?' she asked.

Another good question. 'That was the work of the demon. They use a different type of magic. Otto called it source energy, like it comes from the very core of the planet, the thing that keeps the world spinning through space. Something like that,' he said as she screwed up her face in bewilderment. 'look, the thing to keep in mind is that Rebecca packs a mean punch. She can generate something called hellfire which she can then throw. Otto says it kills. I got hit by it and I can tell you it hurts.

Gitta shook her head, she had to have misheard him or misunderstood something. 'You just said it kills but then said you got hit by it. What am I missing?'

'Ah, yeah. I'm kind of immortal.'

She just looked at him.

'There was an incident when I was in the demon place with the wizard. I got immortalised. Or whatever the right term might be. I think,' he added which didn't help to clarify things at all.

Time was ticking on and they were still at the diner. She listed what Zachary had told her as bullet points as she went. 'The Kochs can do magic. They are enslaved to a demon called Rebecca who has a smoking hot body and is probably insane and they can all do magic. The Kochs might not be all that handy with it but will try to shoot us to make up for that and if Rebecca makes hellfire, get out of the way or die. Is that about it? Oh, one more thing, you're immortal.'

Zachary said, 'That's about it. Now we need to find them. Where would they go?'

Gitta shrugged, trying to get on board with his positive attitude but feeling defeated. 'Back to their place? To the old barracks already? They could have gone anywhere; they own most of the buildings in a twenty-kilometre radius.'

'Then we start at their place. Get some clothes but make it something you can take off easily. We are going hunting.' He wanted to follow up with a clever comment about her clothes and general nakedness that would hint at the fun he hoped they might have later when all this was behind them. He had found another shifter and now he had seen her naked and she was sexy as all hell. He could stay here; he could get to know her. With the Kochs gone, he might be able to settle into a place like this. It was remote and quiet, and he already had a job. Now was not the right time for jokes though.

As he had done two nights ago, he gave her a minute to get upstairs and then went up himself. His clothes were where he had left them, jeans, a t-shirt and his spare pair of boots. He would try to retrieve his other boots later; they were much newer, and it wasn't easy finding them in his size.

Her hurried movements could be heard from his room and he knew when she was back out in the hallway that ran through the upper floor of the diner. As he came out of his room, she was jogging along the corridor. Her tears were gone, and she looked ready to bust heads. This was more like it.

'Ready?' he asked.

She was past him though and heading down the stairs. 'I need to find my little girl, Zac. I need her back and I need that to happen now.' She stopped at the bottom of the stairs and he almost bumped into her he was following so close behind. To his great surprise she leaned into him, reached up with one hand and pulled his face down towards hers.

The kiss was short; no more than a meeting of lips, but it ignited a fire in him. 'You don't have to help me, Zac. This isn't your fight, I know that.'

'It is now,' he argued.

She put a finger to his lips to stop him talking. 'You ought to go, but you won't, will you? I get that now. I thought maybe you were just helping me to get into my pants, but that's not it at all. You want that, but that's just biology. You want to help because you see someone who needs helping. That's it, isn't it?'

She took the finger away and he caught her hand with both of his as he looked into her eyes. 'That and they took a little girl. I don't like injustice and I don't like people who use their power over other people for their own gain. When I left the bar with them on Friday night, I thought I could scare them away, or hurt them enough that they elected to leave and never come back. I was wrong though. I feel like ...'

'Stop,' Gitta interrupted him. 'If you are about to say Horst Koch taking Paula and my mum is because of you, then you are mistaken. This showdown has been coming for a long time. Everyone else here gave into their pressure a long time ago. I think I have been this stubborn because of my shifter nature. Mum wanted to sell up and move on years ago. Come on, I want to see if they are at home. We can surprise them there.'

They still had the Kochs' Mercedes pickup truck but they couldn't drive it all the way back to the farm. Doing so would announce their presence when they wanted to approach stealthily. It was a terrible balance; they had no idea if the Kochs had just gone home with their captives or not, but if they rushed in to get their answer, they would lose the element of surprise. However, to get the element of surprise they needed to approach slowly which would waste time that could be spent looking elsewhere if indeed the Kochs and Gitta's family were not there.

They had to start the search somewhere, so they went back outside, and this time Zac jumped in the driver seat and started the engine. Gitta had left the keys in it in her haste to get inside, and now she stood staring at him open mouthed.

'You lied!' she squawked at him. 'You lied about being able to drive just so I would change into human form.

He tried to stop the grin but there was no way he could hold it back. 'It was totally worth it,' he admitted. She was staring at him with red cheeks and her hands balled on her hips. 'Come on, saucy. It's time to go.'

Muttering about men and how anything with a penis was to be considered trouble, she got in the passenger side with a scowl and continued scowling at him for the next five minutes, only dropping it when she pointed to a dirt track and said, 'Pull in there.'

A hundred metres up the track, they were hidden from view, but Zachary broke a few branches off nearby trees to help disguise the car anyway. The last thing he wanted was for the Kochs to find it and claim it back now.

Wordlessly, they both stripped, each putting their clothes back on their seats before Zachary locked the car and hid the keys in the nook of a branch too high for anyone to see. All the while Gitta was taking off her clothes, he kept his eyes averted. He had seen it now. He wanted to see it again, but that would come later if he was lucky. Staring at her now would just make her uncomfortable.

Gitta noticed that he wasn't staring. It surprised her in a way. He was clearly heterosexual and attracted to her. She had been ready for him to comment that she wasn't wearing a bra. Knowing that she was going to shift, the last thing she wanted was awkward clasps and things to mess around with. She could manage without the support for a few hours.

She couldn't help stealing a glance at him though, his muscular butt was most impressive, but then so was every other part of him. He was quite the specimen, and she couldn't help but wonder what it might be like to have his skin pressed up against hers.

Pushing the unwelcome and errant thought from her mind, she remembered her missing daughter and pushed herself to change. A moment later Zachary changed too and the pair of them set off through the woodlands. Gitta had lived here all her life and could find the Kochs' place without needing to orientate herself.

The three-kilometre journey on foot took them just less than five minutes, their supernatural strength matched by supernatural speed as they ran without pause in a straight line. Jumping fences and hedgerows when they came to fields, they were soon approaching the farm from the far side, away from the road where a sentry might be watching.

They saw no one and heard nothing and soon discovered there was no one to see or hear. The farm was deserted. The first place Zachary checked was the barn. Not that he expected to find Hans still there but it was good to be thorough and since they were going past it and that would put it behind them, he made sure it was empty so no one could shoot them in the back. Inside, he found the chains they used earlier. They were in a box now, packed up next to some other items as if ready to be used later. He picked them up quickly to inspect them, remembering how impossible they were to escape from. It gave him an idea.

As it became obvious the farm was deserted, Zachary swore, voicing the disappointment they both felt. 'We need to check the house,' he said as he went toward a door. 'Just because their cars aren't here, doesn't mean they haven't left people behind with Paula and Meg.'

Gitta knew he was right, but she also knew her daughter wasn't here. She could tell instantly, but whether that was a mother's instinct or something supernatural, she had no idea. She still wanted to search the house though, if one of the brothers was here then they could take a hostage of their own, or maybe just reduce the Kochs' numbers.

Inside, they found no trace of anyone and there was no warmth to the kettle or the stove, so they had been gone for hours. It was a total bust at this location.

'Where next?' he asked. 'Do they own another place where you think they might go?'

Reluctantly, she shook her head. 'There's too many to choose from.'

'Then maybe we head to the barracks. I wouldn't mind getting a look around before they lure us there later. It would help if we were familiar with the layout of the place. Do you know it well?'

'I played there a few times as a kid. We all did at some point. There are holes in the fences so we would get in and ride our bikes and skateboards and see which buildings we could get into.'

Zachary drew in a lungful of air, breathing it out slowly through his nose as he considered his next move. 'They mean to lure us into a trap. I think we should set them a trap of our own.'

Chapter 24

They wanted to make sure they didn't stand out which meant ditching the SIA car before they got anywhere near the target. The three antennae poking up from the tail end of the roof might not be overt but to anyone paying attention they were a clear indication that the car came with heightened communications equipment and that usually meant cops. They weren't cops, not really, but the difference was insignificant.

'So, how are we getting there?' asked Mailer, confused about parking the car. They were in Soltau, a spa town fifteen kilometres from Bad Dorstel and the two men he travelled with were heading into the town centre now, not to the train or bus station. 'Hey, guys, we don't have time to stop for sightseeing,' he called as he hurried after them. The dynamic was very much them and him, but he wasn't going to put up with any crap and find himself in hot water because these two thought it would be okay to goof off.

Neither man paid him any attention, walking past shops and restaurants as if they knew where they were going. He trailed after them, all the way through the short business area until the nicely displayed stores gave way to lower-rent businesses where they started paying more attention to the windows.

At a second-hand clothes shop, Kiel tapped his partner, Kretchmann, on the arm before crossing to the door and leading him inside.

Getting angry, mostly at himself for being unable to do anything about their current course of action, he arrived inside to find them both holding up garments. 'What are you doing now?' he asked, doing his best to sound authoritative though he worried it came out whiney.

'Check the mirror,' instructed Kiel. 'What do you look like?' Mailer looked down at himself, wondering what Kiel was asking him but it had been a rhetorical question. 'You look like a cop. You are wearing sensible cop shoes and cheap trousers that have been neatly pressed. We are going into a farming community and the best way to not have everyone look at us and instantly stop talking because we look like cops, is to ... not look like cops,' he finished his own sentence.

Then Kretchmann walked over with a pair of brown trousers, they looked like they were made from hopsack and would be about as comfortable as wearing hessian. He held them up to Mailer's waist. 'These should fit you. Find a coat as well, something old and either stained or faded; no one wears anything with any value to work a muddy field.'

Kiel threw him a gaudy purple square of material. 'Here, make a shawl or something out of that. Or find an old hoody to wear beneath the coat - we have to cover up your hair, it's far too neat.'

Ten minutes later, the three men stepped back out on the street wearing their new clothes. Kiel had a receipt to claim back expenses, but they had only spent twenty-three Euros to clothe all three of them. Walking back through the town centre and its nice shops, they attracted a few looks because now they looked out of place. Mailer felt self-conscious but kept his mouth shut because he knew they were right; they would blend in now when they got to Bad Dorstel. Kiel and Kretchmann even had a plan to get there, hopping on a bus going that direction with an intention to either walk the last couple of kilometres or hitch a lift on a passing farm vehicle if they could. The new clothes even hid their weapons well.

It was warm on the bus and by pure luck they found themselves sat next to a gaggle of women who were on their way back to Bad Dorstel. Since it was Sunday, they worked a half day and had travelled by bus to Soltau where they could shop and get a coffee or whatever immigrant farmworkers did with their money.

The most startling thing was the change in Kiel and Kretchmann. Surly and grumpy toward him every minute of their journey so far, the moment they got on the bus and saw the women, they transformed into two chatty, happy guys with anecdotes to exchange. They were flirting and smiling and asking questions. Mailer tried to join in but while it seemed to flow naturally for his companions, he felt awkward and out of place. After a couple of minutes of joining in, he chose to just face forward and keep quiet, listening in to their conversation.

'We need work, that's the long and short of it,' claimed Kiel. 'We were working at a Christmas tree place in December, that was okay work if you don't mind the pine sap. That was just outside Hamburg and for the last couple of months we found jobs at a factory packing boxes. It's pretty miserable work, but it's in the warm. I don't mind the cold so much, but my little brother,' he grabbed Mailer's head and gave it a shake, 'he's a bit of a wimp,' some of the women giggled or made sympathetic noises, 'so I try to get him a job inside in the winter.'

'Spring is here though,' announced Kretchmann. 'So, the warm weather will be along any day and who wants to be inside working a desk job then?'

'Where are you heading?' one of the women asked.

Mailer could almost hear the cheeky wink in Kiel's voice. 'I'm planning to follow you to Bad Dorstel. That's where you said you work, isn't it?'

'Is there work there?' asked Kretchmann, getting involved.

In less than five minutes of being on the bus, they knew where they were likely to find work with accommodation on the side and who would pay the best. Their best shot at a job was with some brothers called Koch. They were always hiring it seemed but they weren't the best payers so they should try some of the other farms first.

The advice from one girl, who then got agreement from all the others, was to be at the diner for breakfast in the morning. Most of the village congregated there it seemed, and they would find work for sure.

'The diner?' confirmed Kiel.

'Yes,' replied the woman. 'It's on the main road through the village. You can follow us, if you like. The bus doesn't go that route but it's not far to walk. The woman that owns it might even let you crash there tonight. It doubles as the village bar.'

Kiel figured it was time to go for broke. They would either know or they wouldn't, and he had established a rapport now. With a glance at Kretchmann, who gave him the smallest of nods, he removed the photograph of Zachary Barnabus from his pocket. He had taken some time to batter the photograph around, sitting on it, rubbing in on surfaces and picking at the corners so it looked like something he had been carrying around for a long time.

Holding it up and feigning disinterest, he said, 'I don't suppose any of you have ever seen my friend Zac, have you? He said he was heading this way, but I lost track of him a few months ago. He's a big guy; more than two metres tall, so you would know if you had seen him.'

The nearest woman squinted at the picture as her friends thrust their heads forward to get a look. This was where they found out if they were wasting their time or not. The truck driver dropped him off but that didn't mean he had stayed there. He might have blown straight through or moved on after one night. In either of those cases, he could be anywhere now, and the trail would be cold again.

His heart skipped with a tiny jolt of adrenalin as he saw recognition in her eyes. 'He works at the diner,' she announced with confidence.

'The diner?' this was the best possible news. 'What kind of work is he doing there?'

'I only saw him a couple of times, but he was serving at the bar on Friday night. He could do the most incredible trick with a beer bottle, opening it with just his thumbnail.'

One of the other girls corrected her. 'He's not there anymore.' Kiel kept his face straight. They might not be sunk yet. 'He had some kind of argument with Gitta, that's the woman who owns the place,' she explained.

'With her mother,' added another woman.

'Yeah, she owns it with her mother. I don't know what the fight was about. Something to do with the Kochs I think, but she was shouting at him in the diner while everyone was having their breakfast. It looked like a lovers' tiff to me.'

Her comment elicited a round of hasty discussion about whether the new man, who they all thought was quite something to look at, might or might not already be bedding the woman at the diner.

Kiel let them argue for a minute but then had to interrupt. 'Did he leave?'

The women turned their attention his way. The one nearest Kiel, the one he had been flirting with said, 'I couldn't tell you, but Gitta seemed pretty mad at him.'

'When was that? When was their fight?'

'Yesterday morning.'

Kiel swivelled around in his seat to face the direction of travel and thought. He knew where Barnabus had been up until thirty something hours ago. This was the closest he had ever been, but if the shifter had moved on already, the journey, the subterfuge, the whole operation was pointless. He wouldn't know until he got there so he had to hope it was a lovers' tiff and they had made up already. That would be par for the course with his girlfriend. She would fly off the handle for no reason he could perceive most times and then give him fantastic apology sex a few hours later. He loved it when she was angry about something and chose to take it out on him.

They were going to the diner and then they would see what there was to see.

Chapter 25

They were less surreptitious about the car this time when they parked it. Gitta was certain no one ever came out this way apart from kids who broke into the old barracks to play as she had done a decade ago.

There were several holes in the fence, a small cluster of wild deer scattering when they heard Zachary tear the fence to make a hole big enough for him to climb through easily. The whole place was completely overgrown, nature laughing at man's attempts to tame the planet as concrete, tarmac and other surfaces were reclaimed by weeds and shrubs and trees. In places, the roots had already begun to break the surface, causing tarmac to crumble. The buildings were still standing but very few windows were left intact; kids most likely throwing rocks to break them despite having no reason to do so.

'How big is this place?' Zachary asked, scanning around to take it all in. It wasn't small, that was for sure, but it wasn't vast either. In the distance, he could see the far fence line; it was perhaps four hundred meters away.

'It's big enough to get lost in,' Gitta replied, starting to cross the barracks away from the fence as she headed for the larger buildings in the centre. 'Ahead of us is accommodation and a parade square. Just to the left,' she pointed, 'is a shop of some kind; I guess they like to be self-contained and give the soldiers everything they needed in one place. Then over there is where I think they kept vehicles. I don't remember ever seeing them, they closed this place down when I was very little but the buildings there have roll up doors for something big to get in and out and there are bits of old trucks left in places. The barracks has been picked clean but there are items too heavy for the kids to shift so they are still here, mostly growing into the ground now though.'

'Any idea where they might set themselves up?'

Gitta touched his arm to stop him. When he glanced down to see what she wanted, she said, 'You know they mean to kill you, right?'

A snort of laughter escaped through his nose. 'I wish them luck with that.' Then he turned serious. 'The mission is to rescue Paula and Meg and get the three of you to safety. They can't handle one werewolf, let alone two. You and I will be able to tear through them. My only concern is Rebecca.'

Quietly, Gitta said, 'I won't be able to change, Zac. I can't let Paula see me like that. I don't know if she is like me; I don't know if that is how this works. You said neither of your parents were shifters, so where does your ability come from? If she isn't like me, and I hope to God she isn't, then I want to protect her from even knowing about it.'

Zachary wanted to argue but wouldn't let himself. It changed things, but ultimately, he had planned to deal with them himself, only considering a new plan when he discovered Gitta's supernatural side.

He said, 'Let's explore,' and held out his hand for her to take.

The barracks took up enough space to hide four city blocks in, but a lot of it was sports pitches or parade grounds or other spaces which they could ignore. Zachary had an idea for what he was looking to find and knew when he saw it.

Fresh tyre tracks running through a patch of soft dirt collected on a corner was a clear indication that someone had been through here in the last day. He figured the Kochs would want to make sure they knew the territory better than their prey so would get in and set up. There was no sign of a vehicle though and no noise to indicate they might still be here. Even so, they approached stealthily, coming up on a large building that turned out to be the gymnasium.

Inside, it was dark, the rooflights and windows long since blackened by years of dirt. A portable generator sat to one side in the main gym area, a large room with raised seating along one wall for spectators to watch the home team win or lose. Cables snaking away from the generators went to lights on tripods so they could illuminate the space later.

Gitta asked, 'Do we sabotage them?'

He almost said yes, but then saw a better plan. 'No. We use them to our advantage. The Kochs are cocky enough to never consider that we might come here beforehand.' He wasn't the kind of person that made plans or devised ideas that would confound his opponents; usually he just walked up to them and hit them until they either begged him to stop or just lost consciousness. Today though, he considered that perhaps a little finesse might be required.

Gitta wasn't doing so good; her missing little girl was with some bad people, people he had then told her could wield magic and would definitely consider murder as an option to solve their problems. He could see she was thinking about Paula now, Gitta's pretty face wracked with misery and fear. He needed to keep her distracted and focused on what they needed to do. So, he outlined his plan and her part in it. Then set her to work while he began to play with the lighting cables.

All too soon, Horst would invite them to walk into his trap and the Kochs could return at any moment. They needed to do what they planned to do quickly and then make themselves invisible. But Zachary was betting on the Kochs wanting to wait until dark so they had Rebecca with them. She would provide a level of protection even Zachary found hard to fight against.

He was wrong though; they didn't wait.

Chapter 26

Kiel was starting to worry that his flirtatious approach, which had got him all the information he wanted, had been just a little too effective. The woman he got most of his information from, who he now knew to hail from Romania, was called Sofia and she was chatting with him as they walked to Bad Dorstel. She wouldn't shut up and was getting quite tactile, touching his arm and smiling at him. A lot.

Mercifully, they reached the farm the women all worked at before they got to the diner, which was another kilometre they said. There, Sofia was dragged away by her companions. She waved and wished the man luck finding work and said she would see him at the diner for breakfast in the morning.

Once the women were out of earshot, Kretchmann asked, 'Did you set a date for the wedding.'

'Get bent.'

'I expect to be best man, you know.'

'Don't rile me, Kretchmann.'

'Just remember to keep a tier of the cake to eat when you christen the first baby.' Kretchmann had to jink away from a swipe as Kiel swung a fist at his ear.

'Dick head,' Kiel growled as his partner revelled in the brief moment of frivolity. Then he turned his attention back to Mailer. 'You're awful quite back there, policeman. Nothing to say?'

'About your girlfriend?' he asked trying to make a joke. It went down like a lead balloon, so he quickly added, 'Shouldn't we start talking strategies? If we find Barnabus our instruction is to call base. Bliebtreu wants to speak to him in person.'

Kretchmann swung around to look at him. 'He didn't say that to us.'

Finally, Mailer felt like he had a superior position. 'He gave the instruction to me in person. I think that's why he sent me along; to make sure his orders were carried out.' Both Kiel and Kretchmann stopped walking and rounded on him, getting into his face.

'Are you saying we can't be trusted?' asked Kiel, jabbing Mailer in the chest.

Mailer slapped his hand away. 'I'm not saying anything.' He could feel his cheeks colouring. 'Bliebtreu wants this handled in a specific way. We are to locate Barnabus but not engage. Bliebtreu can be here in a few hours. As soon as we confirm he is here, I will contact him.'

Kiel narrowed his eyes and leaned in so his face was only a few centimetres from Mailer's. 'You do what you want to, sheriff. Kretchmann and I have been tracking supernatural creatures since the SIA formed. So, we'll find him and then we'll see if he wants to cooperate.'

A rebuke made it to his lips, but Kiel and Kretchmann had already turned away and were walking again. 'Hey.' He growled at them. This wasn't how it was supposed to be. He was the law enforcement officer and he wasn't used to being disrespected.

They didn't slow down though, Kretchmann choosing to walk backward a few paces so he could give Mailer the bird.

Seething but impotent, Mailer stared at the sky and considered calling Bliebtreu now. The boss would want to know, but it wasn't how things were done and both Kiel and Kretchmann were well liked and respected by the other agents at the SIA whereas Mailer was still an unknown, unproven rookie. If he reported their behaviour to Bliebtreu what could he even say, 'I think they might do something they shouldn't?' It would just make him look weak and foolish and earn him the condemnation of the wider team.

Wishing he had something he could vent his frustrations on, he swallowed his pride and started after them, jogging to catch up and hoping they wouldn't screw with him too much.

Luckily, the diner was in sight, a pole with a beer sign on it visible even from half a kilometre away. Kiel and Kretchmann were too focused on that to care about Mailer. As he caught up to them, both men had their weapons out, checking they were loaded and safe even though they already knew they were.

Then, with the guns tucked back into the pockets of their old coats, they approached the building as casually as they could.

Chapter 27

Zachary had just finished putting things in place and making sure they were hidden when he heard a car door shutting outside. Gitta heard it too, both whipping their heads around to check with each other. Neither imagined it though and their escape route back out the main entrance was now cut off.

Voices increased his sense of alert; they were coming their way and would discover them in seconds. It would ruin any chance they had to tip the element of surprise. Gitta grabbed his hand, yanking him after her and away from the voices as she headed deeper into the gym. It was still dark, light from the entrance barely penetrating and it was only that their night vision had adjusted that allowed them to see.

She led him to a door set into the wall of the gym. Whether she knew where it went or was just getting them out of sight he didn't know, but they slipped through just as Horst came into the gym, his unmistakeable voice giving his brothers instruction to get set up. The small sound of a frightened child reached his ear and he knew Gitta heard it too because she tensed and tried to go back. She knew her daughter was in there and she wanted to see her, to tell her mummy was coming. It wasn't the right time for that though and as she fought to get around him, Zachary had to clamp a hand over her mouth and carry her away.

'Not yet,' he begged, holding her tight so she couldn't flail against him. 'Soon, I promise. We have to play this right. They won't be expecting it and they have done us a favour by getting here early. The sun doesn't go down for thirty minutes yet. We can spring their trap before they have any chance of being aided by Rebecca.'

Gitta sagged in his arms. She knew he was right. They had gone over what they wanted to do and how it might or might not play out a dozen times. She had done her best to focus on the task, not let her mind wander to dwell on how Paula might be feeling. She was with her grandmother, that was something, but she didn't know the men and Gitta was certain her little girl would be terrified.

'Sorry,' she apologised though she knew he wasn't looking for her to. 'It's just …'

'I know,' he told her, giving her hand a squeeze. 'We are getting her back.' Then he continued through the dark passage, leading Gitta to a right turn that took them by changing rooms and toilets and a large open space that had probably once been an equipment store. Navigating in his head, Zachary was not surprised when the passage led them back out to the main entrance. Cautiously opening a door, he peered out into the lobby.

Light from the early evening flooded into the dark space from outside to be eaten up just a metre in, but the sudden noise of the generator starting up was followed by light coming the other way. They had the portable spotlights working. It had to be now. They needed to go in to disturb the Kochs before they could get fully set up. Whatever they had planned would suffer from his interruption, so he let go of Gitta's hand and pulled off his t-shirt.

He didn't bother to ask if she was ready when he kicked off his boots, it wasn't something a person could ever really be ready for and they were going anyway.

'Just wait for the right moment and get Paula and your mum to safety. Don't look back, okay? I'll be fine. I'll meet you at the diner. Tomorrow the Kochs will be gone and you can get back to normal life.'

'Don't change,' she said, stopping him just before he closed his eyes to begin his transformation. He looked at her questioningly; they needed to get going, but she leaned into his space, just like she had before, back at the diner, and she kissed him. This time though, there was a good deal more heat to it and it wasn't over in under a second like the first time. In the end, he broke the kiss, standing up to shift forms because he was naked, and things were starting to happen a metre south of his mouth.

Once the change was complete, the top of his head was scraping the ceiling in the small lobby, but he felt good. It was a powerful form to be in. His werewolf body was vastly stronger than his human one, which was pretty damned strong anyway, but imbued with supernatural power, he was able to flip cars with one hand and cut through steel with his claws. There would be no thoughts of mercy or leniency this time. It would end here just as soon as he could get Gitta and her family to safety.

He took a pace forward but glanced down at his right hand as Gitta placed hers into it and they walked into the trap like that, hulking werewolf hand in hand with a petite woman.

Horst laughed when he spotted them. They were early, which was annoying, but it was his own fault. He should have told her he would message her later with a location, not tell her where he was going to be. He begged Rebecca for more power last night when the werewolf was unconscious. His brothers had been tending to Hans, who was going nuts about his missing hand and couldn't be trusted to behave, so it was just him and Peter in the barn and he paid no mind to Peter at the best of times.

Rebecca had given him something he was desperate to use. He would kill the stupid werewolf with it. And then he would kill Gitta and her whole annoying family. Peter would complain but Horst was almost at the point where he thought killing his youngest brother might not be a bad idea.

He was the best of them, Horst knew that with utter certainty. The eldest, the brightest, the most capable. He had built their empire and he had found Rebecca, or rather, she had found him but that wasn't the way he told it. Now she had made him even more powerful than ever and told him about the fight that was to come and how after the demons won, loyal servants would be rewarded with a fiefdom or territory within the demon's territory that he would have dominion over. His own kingdom if you will. That was her promise to him, and he didn't need any of his brothers for that. They were entirely expendable.

His brothers hadn't even noticed the werewolf and Gitta yet, they were all so numb to the world around them.

When the little girl cried, 'Mommy!' Only then did they look up.

Horst folded his arms and stared at the couple approaching. He felt superior and in control - as it was supposed to be. 'I haven't called you yet. Your instructions were to wait for me to message you.'

'We got impatient,' Zachary replied.

The brothers were a flurry of movement, dashing to take up pre-planned positions Zachary thought, which he had anticipated but he hadn't expected what Hans did. When Paula spotted her mother approaching and called out to her, Gitta tensed again; an involuntary reaction she could not have prevented, but Zachary held her in check. It was a good thing he did because Hans pulled a gun and pointed it right at the little girl's head.

Gitta wailed in her fright, 'No!'

Horst glanced at his one-armed brother and back at Zachary and Gitta. 'Oh, don't worry, Gitta. Just think of it as an insurance policy in case your big friend gets any bright ideas.'

Meg, who was being held in place by Manfred just behind Hans and Paula, shouted, 'Leave her alone! Curse you Horst; curse you all, you evil...'

Her rant was cut off by a swift pistol whip as Hans glanced and struck. Her head rocked back, and she threatened to keel over, staying upright only because Manfred held her there. Blood trickled from a ruined lip.

Hans put the gun back against the little girl's head. 'Got any smart comments this time, wolf boy?' he sneered, loving the sense of power he felt.

Keen to get on with things, but making time for some theatrics, Horst raised his arms to indicate about the gymnasium. 'How do you like the setting I chose?' He wore a beaming smile that Zachary wanted to cut off. 'No one from the village will disturb us here, Gitta. We can conduct our business quietly and calmly and move on with our lives. I would have happily done this over a drink in your bar, but you continually refused to see reason.'

Gitta wanted to point out that he was forcing her to hand over her business at gunpoint, but he already knew that, and she wasn't sure her voice would hold steady if she tried to talk. She couldn't take her eyes off Paula; her little girl was weeping silently and should never have been exposed to anything like this.

'Did you bring the deed to the diner?' Horst asked.

Gitta reached into her back pocket to produce the crumpled paperwork. Holding it aloft she said. 'I just want my family back. Take the diner and let us go. We'll drive into the sunset and you'll never see us again.'

Horst nodded as if her proposal was acceptable. 'That is a wise course of action, Gitta. A little late, but wise, nevertheless. Before we get to that though, I'm afraid we must deal with the rather deadly companion you brought with you.'

Zachary tensed; they were going to have to do it soon. Or they might miss their chance. If he was incapacitated; chained up or whatever, then the Kochs would be able to do whatever they wanted. Hans had the girl though, and Zachary didn't see how he could enact their plan while she had a gun to her head; it was just too risky.

Horst was staring at Zachary, in fact, all the Kochs were and they were all smiling. 'Were you perhaps hoping to spring the trap you set for us?' Horst asked, the smile never leaving his face. 'We found the kill switch you wired into the lights. We also found the trip wires you set up so we couldn't chase the women as they fled. That was the plan, wasn't it? Kill the lights, then rush us. No doubt the werewolf planned to kill us all while you escaped with your family Gitta.'

Gitta felt sick. The plan was always a shaky one but neither she nor Zachary believed the Kochs were going to let her live, so they had no choice. 'It's was just a precaution,' she lied. 'Just in case you didn't keep your word. I just want to take my family and leave.' She was close to begging now, watching her daughter constantly try to escape from the mangled arm that held her in place and the cruel pistol muzzle digging into the top of her head.

'Good, Gitta. I feel you that you finally understand your position in the village. You can take your mother and daughter as soon as you sign over the deeds. But ...' he raised his voice just as she started to move, 'not until after we have chained your beast. We will deal with him when you are gone. There's no need for the little girl to see it; we are not total monsters.'

Gitta had a hundred responses on her lips but she bit them all down as she looked up at Zachary. He leaned down to whisper in her ear. 'Go. I'll see you back at the diner. I'll bring the deeds with me.'

Then he let go of Gitta's hand and walked away from her. The pile of chains on the floor had been visible the moment he came in. He had expected this and knew being chained up would guarantee him a lot of pain in the near future. It wouldn't stop him from killing them though. He was going to kill them all.

At the chains he knelt, putting both knees on the floor. Gitta was crossing the room toward Horst, the diner's deeds in her hand. To bring attention back to him, he raised his voice and called out. 'Now, Horst. This can go one of two ways.'

'Let me guess,' chuckled Horst. 'The easy way or the hard way.'

'Ha! No, Horst. No, there is no easy way. You waved that goodbye a long way back. No, your options are to kill yourselves in as painless a way as you can devise. Or I rip you to shreds and dip the bits in vinegar. Vinegar on cuts really stings.' He added in case they hadn't understood.

Rolf came up next to Zachary and pointed a handgun at his temple. 'Don't move.' Then Peter, looking nervous as always, and keeping his eyes cast down, moved in and started clamping the manacles in place. His ankles first, then his wrists which Zachary had placed behind his back to make it easy for the youngest Koch. Just as Peter went to attach the restraining chain between them, Zachary twitched and shouted, 'Boo!'

Like a terrified rabbit, Peter darted away, squealing with fright. It made his brothers laugh, all except Horst who just shook his head. Even Zachary laughed, which to the brothers seemed incongruous. Didn't he realise they were going to torture him and hand him over to Rebecca? When he escaped earlier, they worried how she might punish them; her instructions to hold him until she could return were very simple. But now they had him again and Rebecca didn't need the whole werewolf. He could go to her missing some parts.

Gitta had reached Horst where he stood by the generator, the harsh spotlight shining down from a high tripod bathing them in enough light to make her hair glow. His hand was held out for her to place the deed into it. She wanted to be the wolf, she wanted to tear at him, but Paula had been through enough without seeing the beast inside her mother, and she couldn't risk the chance that Hans might actually shoot her.

Horst took the deed wordlessly, then looked across to Rolf and Peter. 'Is he secure?'

Rolf backed away a pace then circled around behind Zachary to check the youngest brother's handiwork. Satisfied, he lowered his weapon and called back. 'Yes.'

Horst nodded in acknowledgement and took his gaze back to Gitta. 'Very well.' He held the deed paperwork aloft, pulling a pen from a back pocket and clicking the end to extend the nib. 'You just need to sign them over to me, Gitta. Write that you transfer ownership, then sign and date it please. I'll have our lawyer make it all legal in the morning when the offices open.'

She complied, quickly scrawling on the paperwork and handing it back. 'Now tell your brother to take that gun away from Paula's head,' she was half begging and half screeching. She could feel the change trying to happen, it had been ever since she saw the brothers holding her mum and daughter ten minutes ago. She was barely able to keep it at bay as her anger, fear, and frustration grew. Now the Kochs had what they wanted, and she needed to get her family to safety. She was coming back to rescue Zachary as soon as she was happy they were out of harm's way, but Hans was still smiling his lecherous smile and none of the brothers were moving.

Horst walked a couple of paces to carefully place the deeds in a document folder. When he turned around again, he was taking off his shirt. Rolf and Peter were doing the same.

'I'm afraid that won't be possible, Gitta.' He crossed his arms and started touching the tattoos there. They lit up from within, a dark red light emanating from them that looked like burning coal beneath his skin. 'I made a promise to my mistress, Rebecca, that I would practice my skills and I would be her loyal servant. In return she imbued me with new powers.'

'You said you would let us go,' Gitta wailed, trying hard to keep the beast inside.

Horst paid her no attention as her eyes darted between him and her daughter. Would Hans do it? If she went for him, would he pull the trigger? She slipped off her jacket.

'Each of these markings is made with demon blood. Through them, we are able to conjure elemental magic. My brothers and I have grown adept at conjuring air and fire but where my brothers find it exciting and fulfilling, I have always wanted more.' Manfred's eyes twitched toward his eldest brother, confused about what he was saying. He couldn't see the new tattoo Horst sported, but Rolf could. Until now their markings were exactly the same, now Horst had a new marking, right across the top of his chest. It was bigger and more complex than any of the other markings they bore.

Rolf was instantly unhappy. 'What is that?' he demanded to know, jerking his gun to point at Horst's chest.

'Do not fret, Rolf. We are still brothers. But I will always be eldest. I will always be the senior member of this family, and I have claimed the lion's share for myself.'

Manfred, his curiosity too great, shuffled around, tugging Meg with him so he could see what Rolf was looking at. 'What is it?' he asked.

Zachary watched the dynamics playing out between the brothers. He hadn't expected the gun to be held on the little girl's head the whole time and had been waiting for his opportunity. He had come to accept it wasn't coming though, so now he was going to have to make one of his own.

Rolf wasn't happy about Horst having something he didn't. He wanted it as well and an argument was threatening to start. 'What does it even do?' asked Manfred, whose mind was blown that there could be more magic for them to learn.

Horst touched the symbol, shuddering from the power surging into him as the tattoo lit up from within. Shouting with his excitement, Horst held out his arms as crackling red light began to spread out from the symbol, arcing down his arms with sparks jumping out of his skin to earth back in again. Then two glowing red orbs formed, one in each hand as he laughed triumphantly. 'I can wield the Earth's source energy, that's what the symbol does. I am invincible now!' Then he thrust his hands outward away from his body at Zachary, sending the two deadly orbs of hellfire fizzing through the air to strike his chest.

The twin blasts threw the werewolf back three metres, his lifeless body tumbling and rolling to land facedown on the dusty wooden floor. Horst beamed with delight, the madness in his eyes there for all to see. 'That is what I can do! No more air or fire. I have the power to take life with my hands.'

Gitta watched him closely, stunned at the power he had been able to wield but his body appeared to be burning up, a light smoke rising from his skin.

His brothers were staring at him in awe. They all wanted what he had, and no one was paying any attention to the dead werewolf. Until he spoke, that is.

'Yeah. You might want to check the warrantee period on that tattoo. I don't think it works the way they advertised.'

Horst's jaw dropped open, but before he could ready more hellfire, Zachary was moving. The chains were gone, and he was too fast for the brothers to stop. As the giant werewolf picked up speed, Horst threw more hellfire, the blasts catching Zachary and making him swear out loud, but it didn't slow him down much.

Rolf saw the giant werewolf coming and stepped back as he raised a fire spell in terror. He stepped on loose soil though and lost his footing, tumbling backward which saved his life. Zachary's claws slashed through the air where his head had been, catching Rolf's forehead to cleave it open but not penetrating the bone of his skull. Blood flowed down over his face and into his eyes causing Rolf to stumble as he attempted to flee.

Hans kept his cool and held the little girl in place, the gun pointing directly into her skull. The werewolf wouldn't dare endanger the girl; if he just kept cool, the werewolf would stop. Zachary wasn't stopping though, he was walking directly toward him, in a straight line, his pace determined but unhurried.

Horst fired yet more hellfire orbs directly into Zachary's chest, but the werewolf, even though he faltered slightly with each strike, just kept on coming. When the next pair of blasts hit high up on his chest, the werewolf flicked his eyes in Horst's direction and mimed yawning. 'Will you stop that?' he asked. 'It's getting to be annoying. Just be patient. I'll be with you soon. I need to deal with Hans first.'

Gitta was cowering by the generator, unable to get to Paula without putting herself in the crossfire but she was in the perfect position to observe Horst and could see that every time he produced hellfire, his skin glowed just a little bit brighter.

Then Zachary brought his eyes back to look at Hans and grinned, rows of diabolical teeth gleaming at him. 'I'll do it!' Hans shouted. 'I'll shoot the little girl. I mean it. Don't you take another step!'

Zachary didn't slow down though. It wasn't so much that he was gambling with her life, more that he believed the Kochs intended to kill her and her mother and grandmother and if he didn't hurry up and get to her, Horst would wake up and switch his target. One touch of hellfire and the little girl would be gone. As far as Zachary was concerned there was no time to lose.

In the last two metres, he asked, 'What did we decide your name was again?'

Hans panicked, the werewolf wasn't stopping so he lifted the gun away from Paula's head, finally giving Zachary exactly what he wanted. Hans fired point blank into the werewolf, but Zachary was too close and too fast. He ducked and jinked and came up with the claws of his right hand extended as they shot toward the ceiling.

'Oh, yeah,' he remembered, skewering Hans through his head as the claws went in under his chin and poked out through the top of his head. 'You're small Koch.'

Zachary stepped around the little girl, placing his body between her and both Horst and Manfred. Manfred still had hold of Meg but having seen what happened to Hans, he shoved her roughly away and darted back a pace to give himself room.

Zachary grabbed Meg's arm just as she was falling away from Manfred and hauled her upright, shoving her behind him like he had the little girl. Then he shouted an urgent command to Gitta, 'Get them out of here! Don't look back.'

Gitta looked into his eyes, just for a heartbeat, enough being said with a look that no words were needed. Then she scooped Paula and ran with her, dragging Meg along behind as they ran for the door.

Rolf had fled, Hans was dead, and Peter was nowhere to be seen. That left Horst and Manfred. Zachary believed he was going to enjoy this. He even felt that he had time enough to gloat. Holding his arms at his sides in a non-threatening pose, he addressed them both. They each had spells conjured and ready, fire dancing in Manfred's right hand, hellfire cracking and fizzing in Horst's but neither attempting to do anything with them, probably, in Zachary's opinion, because they knew how little impact they would have.

He didn't mention it, but Horst's skin looked like it was beginning to crack. He was glowing, sort of, which could just be due to the light from the spotlights combining with the glow from his tattoos, but he didn't look good. He looked like he was struggling. Then Zachary worked out what Horst's strained expression reminded him of. Horst looked like he needed to poop.

'The kill switch you found?' he reminded Horst. 'That wasn't a kill switch. I don't know how to do electrics. I just cobbled together some stuff from the box next to the generator and attached it to the cable. I didn't even think it looked all that convincing but there was one thing I was sure of.' He waited for them to ask him what it was, but neither did. It spoiled his punchline a little, but he went for it regardless. 'That you are all as dumb as a bucket of cocks. All this nonsense about ruling a village? Why couldn't you have just helped the local people and paid the migrant workers a fair wage. Anyway, the kill switch thing was to make it look like we had attempted to set some kind of trap. I hoped you would find it, I even made sure I left footprints next to it so you would look there. That way you wouldn't look too hard at anything else. I tampered with the chains when I went to the farm this afternoon. I had no idea if you would use them again, but you knew they would hold me so I figured you probably would. Why change a tactic that works?'

'What are you going to do now?' asked Manfred.

'Manfred, isn't it?' Zachary asked, keeping his tone conversational. It was the first time he had spoken to this brother and he took a half pace forward so he could offer his right hand to shake congenially.

Caught off guard, Manfred automatically dropped his spell and extended his own right hand.

Zachary snatched it, gave it a yank to pull the man off balance, and slashed with his left hand, slicing through Manfred's throat almost all the way back to his spine. He was dead before he hit the floor.

'That's what I'm going to do now, dummy,' he said to the limp form by his feet.

Horst needed no second warning, he loosed both hellfire blasts at Zachary and ran for the main entrance. The hellfire knocked him back but only for second. He could catch Horst easily, but when Zachary gave chase he only got halfway across the gymnasium when someone coming through the door made him pull up.

It was Rebecca and she had Gitta, Meg, and Paula with her.

Chapter 28

It became quickly obvious there was no one at the diner. They knocked and waited and listened and checked for lights on upstairs but even though there was a van parked around the back, there was no one home.

The diner was locked but that didn't stop Kiel and Kretchmann for long. They jimmied a ground floor window open and slipped inside without doing any damage. Mailer waited at the back door as instructed, then, after a minute, he had to wonder if they were coming to let him in or just messing with him.

Just as he was about to accept that he was the butt of another joke, a shadow appeared. Kretchmann opened the door before vanishing back inside without speaking. Mailer was glad to be doing something that felt more familiar. Not the breaking and entering bit, that was completely illegal no matter what badge you carried unless you had justifiable cause, which they did not. They were going to search the house for evidence though and that was a process he knew.

Not that he got much chance to show it. Heading through the house to find their stairs, guessing that the best place to look would be the bedrooms; if Barnabus had possessions here they could assume he was still in the area and wait for him. However, Kretchmann was already on the stairs and Kiel was ahead of him. Kiel shouted back down, 'We'll take the upper floor. See what you can find down there.'

Once again, Mailer had to bite his tongue. He was the one who knew this process, but, he acknowledged, it wasn't that specialist of a skill that the two former soldiers couldn't

have been taught it at some point. Arguing would be churlish and pointless, so he didn't
bother.

That was how he came to be the one who found the note.

When Kiel and Kretchmann came back downstairs looking pleased with themselves
because they had found what had to be Barnabus's clothes and belongings, Mailer was
doing as he so often saw them do, and nonchalantly checking over his sidearm.

'He's still here,' announced Kiel, always the chattier of the two. 'His stuff is in a room
upstairs. You find anything?'

'The note,' Mailer said, nodding at it with his head as he stared down the deconstructed
barrel of his gun. 'They are at an old barracks nearby. It's about a kilometre and a half to
the west. If we hurry, we should be able to get there for dark.'

Kiel and Kretchmann hurried over to read the note. 'It doesn't say who it is from,' Kiel
pointed out.

Without looking up, Mailer slotted his trigger guard back into place, completing the
rebuild of his handgun and said, 'I hardly think that matters. It would appear that we
have wandered, inadvertently, into some local trouble. The note tells me there is a woman
and a little girl in trouble and that is where Barnabus is going to be. We have a duty to
locate Barnabus, which we appear to have done, I called Bliebtreu already, so he is on his
way here now.'

Kretchmann started forward, instantly angry that Mailer had gone over their heads to
contact the boss. He wanted to be the one to bring the werewolf in. Kiel stopped him with
an arm to his chest. It would achieve nothing if the damage was already done. Besides,
it was a four-hour drive for Bliebtreu to get to them. They could have the whole thing
wrapped up nice and neat to deliver to him by then.

Mailer continued, 'We also have a moral obligation to help the woman and the little girl.
I don't think local boys, if that's what this is, will give you two hard-asses much trouble.'
He said it with a casual smile, paying them a compliment at exactly the right time and
it worked. They didn't fight him on his desire to help the victims. Mailer slid the last

component into place, made sure it locked home, and checked the action before standing up. 'How about if I help you gentlemen apprehend a couple of local criminals. If along the way, we accidentally find Barnabus and take him into protective custody, well I don't think the boss could be too upset about that, could he?'

Now both men actually smiled at him, surprised by his attitude and wondering if perhaps they might have misjudged him.

There was nothing more to say. They knew their drills and had some territory to cross on foot so there was no time to waste. Back outside, they ditched their coats and shawls. The sun was almost set, and it would be full dark soon, disguises wouldn't be necessary if they caught up to Barnabus in the next few hours. With Kretchmann leading the way, the three of them set off at a steady jog to cover the distance to the target.

Chapter 29

The sun had set. In the time it had taken Zachary to gain the upper hand, the sun had gone down and now Rebecca was here. Gitta, Meg, and Paula must have run into her outside, escaping the Kochs only to run into an equal if not worse problem.

Rebecca looked at Horst and then at Zachary behind him and then across at the bodies of Manfred and Hans lying under the temporary spotlights. 'It would seem that I have missed much.' She was clearly displeased. Hellfire crackled in her left hand as she held Gitta's neck in her right. Gitta held Paula and was doing her best to hide the little girl's face from the dead bodies littering the gymnasium floor.

'Good evening, Rebecca,' Zachary hallooed her jovially with a wave. 'I'm afraid your Koch ration is a little depleted. I was forced to kill a couple of them. If you could just go back outside and give me a minute or so, I'll finish the job and then we'll be out of your hair. Okay?' He gave her what he hoped was a cheesy grin and a double thumbs up.

She frowned as she uttered, 'I grow tired not only of your perpetual jabbering, but of your defiance. I am a god among insects, beast.' Then she lifted her left hand and let the hellfire fly from it.

Zachary knew it was coming, huffing out a breath the moment before it hit him though it still knocked the wind out of him. The single ball of hellfire had more juice to it than both of Horst's combined. Thrown backward two metres, he landed in a press up position, fingers and toes to the floor and nothing else. Just for good measure he performed a couple of press ups, watching Rebecca's face as her eyes widened.

Gitta sensed the demon's distraction and carefully, but insistently, pushed Paula across to her mother. Then, with Rebecca still holding her neck, she slowly slipped off her boots, first the left then the right. The demon didn't seem to notice.

'How?' Rebecca stared at Zachary. 'No human can survive hellfire. None ever has. How are you still alive?'

Zachary saw Rebecca's hand slip from Gitta's neck as she took a pace toward him. Fresh hellfire formed in both of her hands and he readied himself for another salvo. Gitta needed a few seconds and he was the distraction.

'Stop!'

The new voice startled everyone. Zachary was poised to dart one way or the other, his muscles tense and bunched. Rebecca packed a lot more punch than Horst, but he would get to her if he could and fight her close quarters. He had gone toe to toe with a demon before and last time he didn't know he would survive, this time he did. Gitta was down to her jeans and stretchy top and had already undone the top snap to wiggle out of her jeans. She didn't want to transform in front of Paula, but she no longer saw an option.

But now all bets were off, because there was a new player in the room.

'What is the meaning of this, Rebecca?' the new arrival asked, stepping into the room so everyone could see him. Zachary recognised him instantly, his handsome face and neatly clipped beard and hair easy to remember.

Rebecca turned toward the newcomer, flicking her hair in annoyance at being interrupted. 'What do you want, Daniel?'

Following Daniel as he strode into the room were more than a dozen shilt, all with their weapons drawn and two of them holding Rolf between them. Rolf's face and whole front half were covered in blood where it had run down from the deep gashes in his forehead.

Gitta spread her arms and used them to guide her mother and daughter backward away from the new threat.

'Hey, douchebag,' Zachary waved and smiled. 'Remember me?' Zachary had met Daniel in the immortal realm when he and Otto travelled there to rescue a girl. He was another demon, and though Zachary wouldn't claim to know much about him, he did know Daniel kidnapped humans to train as familiars. Not only that, Daniel now had Otto as his own familiar after Otto killed the one he kept previously. Zachary found he was genuinely curious about how that was going; Otto wasn't the sort that played along.

Daniel looked at him for the first time, cocking his head to one side as if dredging his memory. 'Ah yes, the annoying werewolf who won't die.'

'Where's Otto?'

Daniel spared the werewolf an annoyed gaze. 'Attending to other matters, shifter.'

'He is immune to hellfire,' blurted Rebecca. 'How is that possible?'

Daniel sniffed and moved yet further into the room, walking past Rebecca as she turned on the spot to watch him. 'A surprising side effect from a fight with Teague is the answer to your question. His immortality, or whatever it is, is of no interest to me though. What you have been doing is.'

'I have done nothing wrong.' she argued.

'Will Beelzebub agree?'

Gitta glanced at the door; there was no way she could get out through it; a dozen ugly creatures with reptilian heads blocked the way. She had no idea what they were, but she was certain they were not friendly.

When Rebecca didn't reply, Daniel continued. 'The practice of familiar marking was outlawed thousands of years ago, Rebecca. No one has dared to perform the rituals since because the familiars never survive. Not for long anyway. The only reason to do it, is to make them into powerful weapons for the brief period that they live.'

Horst chose that moment to voice his concerns. 'Mistress, I don't feel so good.'

Rebecca swung her head to look at him, but it was Daniel who answered. 'I dare say you do not. I'm afraid you are about to die. You put the *consumnus* mark on him, Rebecca. How did you expect him to survive that? No human can survive for more than few hours once they start channelling hellfire.' Casually, almost without looking, in fact, Daniel raised his left hand and blasted Horst across the room with a single bolt of hellfire. Horst's ragged body crunched into the gymnasium wall ten metres away, hitting it two metres up before dropping to a dead heap on the floor. Then he nodded to the shilt, the two holding Rolf moving in on either side to clamp their faces onto his neck. Rolf shrieked with pain as his life force was sucked out. He writhed and struggled for a few seconds but that was all it took for the fight to go out of him. Then the shilt released his lifeless body and it collapsed to the floor.

Daniel asked, 'Are there any more, Rebecca?'

'Damn you, Daniel,' she spat.

'Hey, guys,' called Zachary to get their attention. 'It's actually way past dinnertime and my pet gerbil gets all kinds of moody if I let him get too hungry. If you're done with us, we'll just let ourselves out.'

Ignoring him, Daniel asked her again. 'Are there any more, Rebecca? Marked familiars are dangerous to us all. They need to be put down, and Beelzebub will want to know why you thought it a good idea to create them in the first place. He might think you were trying to create your own army to stand against him.

Unable to contain her anger any longer, Rebecca brought forth hellfire, firing two blasts at Daniel from less than a metre away so fast he couldn't stop the attack from happening. The proximity of the blast and the low height it came from lifted him off his feet to fire him across the large room. He might have hit the far wall but directly behind him was the portable generator. His body collided with it, toppling it and yanking out a cable somewhere because all the lights winked out. Little Paula squealed in fright at the sudden blanket of nothingness that enveloped her, but Zachary could see just fine.

Instantly, the shilt scattered. Some of them running outside and away from her as she aimed her next shot in their direction and some running at Gitta, Meg, and Paula where the chance of a meal proved too tempting to resist.

Zachary burst into action, thrusting forward with his right leg and slicing into Rebecca as he passed her. He had to cover fifteen metres to get to the shilt before they got to the little girl but Gitta was already moving to block them.

All the shilt saw was a small woman they could easily devour, but as she vanished beneath a pile of them Zachary's direct course to her went sideways, a blast of hellfire from Rebecca knocking him from his feet and into a spotlight tripod as he lost control.

Tumbling down, even as he tried to right himself, Zachary heard when Daniel regained his feet. An enraged roar came after an echo of hellfire as he blasted the portable generator out of his way. Daniel was back on his feet and that gave Rebecca something else to focus on as he started pounding her with hellfire. The two demons lit the room with the light from their exchange, not that Zachary needed it to see, but as he leapt back to his feet, he got to see the shilt on top of Gitta flung backward as the enraged werewolf got back to her feet. A dead-looking shilt hung from one fist and blood dripped from her jaws where she had fought tooth and nail to get out from under the pile of reptilian shilt bodies pinning her down.

He couldn't help but grin. But now was not the time to rest and enjoy the show, there were shilt to kill and there were few things sweeter to his mind than ripping through creatures that seemed to have no purpose other than to prey on people.

There weren't many left but as Gitta scared off one that was threatening her mother and daughter, he saw there were more important things to do than gratify himself. He needed to get Meg and Paula to safety, Gitta too for that matter as the hellfire blasts were still lighting up the room like strobes going off.

The biggest danger, as he tried to get them to the exit, was a loose blast from either one of the demons. He couldn't kill them, but he figured he didn't need to; he could get away with just incapacitating them for a few seconds. Which is what he did.

It was right about now that he missed having the wizard around. Otto had all manner of cool tricks he could employ in such a situation. He wasn't here though, so it was all on him and he had his own cool thing to do.

'Magic,' he muttered as he picked up the cable for the portable generator. 'You can stick your magic right up your butts.' He swivelled off one foot, yanking the cable so the generator jumped off the floor and then he spun, swinging the whole thing around in a wide arc like a hammer thrower at the Olympics. With a grunt, he lined up and yelled, 'I prefer brute force!' The one hundred and fifty kilo lump of engine, prescribed a wide arc, picking up speed as it swept across the room.

At the last gasp, Rebecca saw it coming, her angry grimace dropping, but the generator smashed into her chest, picking her up without the slightest dip in speed as it continued its journey toward Daniel.

He got the warning she didn't though, and as the giant hammer passed through the point he had occupied, it hit nothing. He had opened a portal back to the immortal realm and fallen backward through it. The generator entered the portal before it could snap shut, the cable getting sliced neatly in two as the boundary between the realms closed on it.

Rebecca bounced, tumbled and slammed into a wall. She wouldn't be down for long, but it would be long enough for him to get the little girl and the others to safety.

With no time to spare on checking the fallen demon, he ran across the room. 'Gitta.'

'Zac,' she gasped. He could see her trying to convince Paula the beast she could see was her mummy, but the little girl was traumatised, and nothing was going to make her let go of her grandmother.

'Let's go,' he insisted, grabbing Gitta's arm. 'Work it out later. Maybe she'll think it was all a bad dream. That demon won't be down for long.' Meg didn't need to be told twice, she was anxious to be elsewhere, so the four of them ran, jumping over the fallen shilt and dodging Rolf's lifeless remains as they got to the exit and ran outside into the cold, starry night and right into the next problem.

Looking over the sights of their guns were three men. The one on the left said, 'Don't move, Barnabus.'

Chapter 30

Kiel, Kretchmann, and Mailer found the abandoned British army base easily enough, the two soldiers were used to memorising topography and navigating through thick woodland, but once inside the base they had to work out where to go and got it wrong several times.

It was noise that drew their attention. What they assumed was the hum of overhead powerlines they discerned was in fact the sound of a small engine running. They got that because the volume changed as they rounded a building.

Then flashes of light followed by booming noises, as if someone was firing energy weapons in a sci-fi film, confirmed where they needed to go. Ahead of them, about forty metres away, a pair of broken doors hung loosely from a large building. Light was coming from inside.

They approached stealthily and with caution, sneaking closer and covering each other's movements over open ground. There was no one else around though. Whatever was happening here tonight, it was all contained inside that building.

Just as they got to the door and formed up to go inside, their target walked out. At least, they all assumed it was their target. They had a photograph of Zachary Barnabus the man, yet this was a werewolf. But actually, it wasn't a werewolf, it was two.

There were two of them, both hulking and huge, one larger than the other but even the smaller one had to be way over two metres tall. They both ducked to get out of the building.

Automatically, Kiel raised his weapon, staring down his sights at the larger creature's centre of mass. He made an informed guess and commanded, 'Don't move, Barnabus.'

The smaller werewolf moved to protect two civilians that exited the building at the same time, a woman and a small girl. He knew Mailer wanted to protect them, and would never argue the point, but he was here to claim a bigger prize.

Unfortunately for Keil, Zachary was way beyond the point where he felt inclined to be nice. 'You have about four seconds to live. If any of you are still pointing your weapons even in the general direction of the little girl by then, I will leave your bodies in the dirt and never think twice about it.'

Mailer thought that as threats go, it was a pretty good one, not least because the giant beast that filled his vision looked more than capable of doing exactly what he said. He pointed his weapon down, letting it hang away to his side in his right hand while he held the left up as a sign of surrender. Kiel and Kretchmann didn't twitch, their guns still trained on the werewolf.

Kiel, who had issued the initial warning was itching to shoot the giant beast. He looked like he could take a couple of bullets and survive, and he wanted to be able to brag that he took down a werewolf.

Mailer saw their faces and knew they were going to go against orders. 'Come on, guys!' he shouted. 'Lower your weapons. Our orders are to find him. Nothing else.'

Neither man lowered their weapon.

Zachary needed no further encouragement. 'Time's up.'

Kiel was the first to fire, but only by a nanosecond. The moment Zachary twitched, he pulled his trigger, aiming for one of the target's big meaty thighs. He wanted to bring it down, not kill it. He would get way more kudos if he brought it in alive.

Kretchmann had seen the unexpected additional target too but the larger one was clearly the threat so the moment it started moving, his gun tracked it. He exhaled half a breath to still himself and gently squeezed his trigger the way he had been taught years ago; the way he did every week in the practice ranges.

Kiel got off three shots as the werewolf ran, leapt and became an inevitability he could not hope to avoid. Each shot hit home, but none of them had any effect on the outcome.

Mailer watched in horror as the scene played out. He had tried to delay them finding their target. The moment he found out Bliebtreu was taking a helicopter to get here he knew they had an hour at most before he would arrive. The boss would come directly to the barracks but an hour had already passed and if he had tried to lead them to any more unlikely spots or stopped to tie his shoelace one more time, they would have known he was up to something. He knew they had their own agenda but couldn't believe they were this trigger happy. He hadn't had the required training to be cleared for field ops yet, but he had read the reports from the werewolf incident in Bremen back in January. The shapeshifters were listed as virtually unstoppable; what would make Kiel and Kretchmann think they could take him on?

Zachary felt the first round clip his leg. It caught the outer edge of his quadricep muscle and bounced off. The second hit him just as he leapt into the air, gouging a hole into the side of his right leg just below and inside the knee. The third was wild, the man reacting to the realisation that he was about to die. It caught him on his abdomen, passing through the fleshy part just above his left hip.

Then the other man fired, his first shot missing completely. Zachary came down from his leap, hauled to earth by gravity where he surprised himself by folding his hand over to punch the man in the face. The effect was still like hitting him with a sack of bricks, but he would live.

He didn't get the chance to deal with the second man, who ought to have got a second shot off by now, because Gitta was already there. With the man's attention on Zachary, he hadn't seen her dart across the few metres that separated them, and he was staring down at her hand now as her claws protruded from his chest.

She had skewered him, and Zachary could tell by the look on her face that she couldn't believe what she had done. The wound might be survivable, but as he watched, the man's head lolled back and he fell away from her, pulling the claws out with his own body weight.

Gitta staggered and Zachary caught her, just as the sweet sound of an approaching helicopter reached Mailer's ears.

Zachary couldn't think of anything to say that would help, all he had in his head were glib comments and they would most likely make things worse. In his arms as he held her, Gitta began to shift back to her human form. Meg ran over to her daughter, bringing Paula, and he handed her off to be with her family as he stood up.

There was a third man standing a few metres away. He hadn't fired a shot and was the only one to heed his warning and lower his weapon. Zachary was seeing red though and he wasn't sure he cared what side the man was on.

Mailer saw the huge werewolf lower the naked girl to the ground and raise its head to pierce him with its glowing red eyes. It was horrifying to look at. Whatever else happened tonight, if he survived, Mailer was quitting the SIA tomorrow.

The werewolf took a step toward him.

Eyes widening in fear, Mailer threw his gun down and raised his hands to show they were empty.

The werewolf took another pace.

'I'm from the Alliance,' he blurted. 'Deputy Commissioner Bliebtreu sent me.'

'I don't care,' the huge monster growled.

'I was supposed to find you, that's all. Bliebtreu wants to speak with you, nothing else. I swear.' Mailer was backing away, his feet moving of their own accord.

Zachary knew that he shouldn't be doing what he was doing, but he wasn't going to kill the man, he was just going to give him a nice scar to remember him by.

The hellfire blast hit Zachary square between the shoulders and threw him into the man as he stalked toward him.

Rebecca!

He had forgotten the damned demon. More than a minute had passed since he hit her with the generator, so she'd had plenty of time to recover. Underneath him, the man whimpered in pain, but Zachary placed a hand on the man's head and shoved it into the dirt as he sprang back onto his feet to face the threat.

Hanging from her hand was Peter, the last of the Kochs. He was conscious, barely, he kept trying to lift his head to look around, but whatever clever hiding place he had run off to hadn't been clever enough.

Rebecca dropped Peter to the ground, where he stayed as she sent two fresh balls of hellfire into her hands. She fired them both, but Zachary ducked his head and ran, both orbs fizzing over his head. He needed to beat on something now and she was it.

'Go!' he bellowed at Gitta. Once again, they were in danger, they just didn't seem to be able to get away from it. He jumped over the huddled forms, a glance showing him Gitta was trying to shift back into werewolf form again. Then, he swatted a hellfire blast, taking it on his left forearm. The arm went numb for a second, but the tactic worked because he was able to keep his pace. Rebecca fired again, this time he jinked to the side to evade the shot, but he was almost there. Two more seconds and he was going to tear her apart. She might be able to recover but he was going to make her suffer first.

He was close enough to see her expression change, anger and defiance replaced by doubt and then fear as she realised she wasn't going to be able to stop him no matter what she did. Just like Daniel, she chose the coward's option, opened a portal and stepped backward through it, snagging Peter's unresisting form as she went.

Zachary tried to take her head off with a swing of his right hand but all he got was thin air as the portal closed. He fell, his overcommitted swing hitting nothing to send him off balance.

Choice swearwords filled the air as he picked himself up.

Then he heard it, the small sound of a child crying. He snapped his head around fearing what he was going to see and praying that he would be wrong.

Gitta was dead.

Chapter 31

Zachary didn't even need to look to know what had happened. He had been running directly at Rebecca and he had ducked or dodged at least one of her hellfire shots. Gitta had been shifting back into her werewolf form so she could help him fight the demon.

A blast of hellfire he had ducked flew onwards to hit her and that was all it took.

He couldn't make his body move. He felt completely empty, so he stared at her lying between her mother and her daughter, both of them weeping uncontrollably.

The searchlight from a helicopter appeared in the night sky. It was still half a kilometre away but getting closer and coming straight for them. Zachary wanted to be angry, he wanted to blame someone and take his frustration and despair out on them, but he knew that he was the one to blame.

If he hadn't come here, if he hadn't chosen to interfere, Gitta would still be alive. His brain supplied him with twenty different things he should say or do, each of them he rejected. Gitta's body needed to be taken back to the diner. That was her home. She needed to be dressed to give her some dignity and then laid to rest appropriately, but who was he to play any part in that? He was just some stranger who turned up two days ago and brought death and destruction with him.

He turned to his right and started walking.

The helicopter touched down as he set off, three men exiting quickly while the pilot stayed inside. They tried to intercept him, doing so carefully and with their arms out to show him they were not armed. One of them was shouting something at him, but he couldn't hear it over the noise of the rotors. Zachary didn't care what they wanted, didn't care what they had to say. He picked up his pace and started running, getting up to a full sprint he thought he might never slow down from as he tried to run away from the image of Gitta; a memory he worried he might never escape.

As he left everyone behind him, his head filled with murderous thoughts. Rebecca had killed her. It might be his fault, but remorse wouldn't stop him from levelling the score if he ever saw her again.

Little did he know, his chance would come.

At the diner, he collected his things, and just like he had so many times before, he started walking.

Chapter 32

B liebtreu glanced about, seeing a woman and a little girl on the ground hunched over something. Barnabus had fled but where were his men? Then he saw them, there was movement near to the woman and girl, he hadn't seen it at first because of the shadows the searchlight was creating and the swirling dust his rotors were kicking up.

'Do we chase, sir?' asked the man to his left.

Bliebtreu considered the question. Special Investigator Voss was one of his best men, if anyone could track Barnabus and convince him to calmly listen, then it was him. Something had gone down here though, his men were down, and he needed to check their condition. He shook his head.

'No. I don't want to risk anyone else. If Barnabus is hostile, he might attack without warning. We need to find out what happened here and then maybe reassess our plan to recruit him. We may have to put him down instead.'

Bliebtreu found Mailer still struggling to get up. He had a concussion, but true to his promise, he quit the next day as soon as the doctor discharged him and was back in Bielefeld and his job less than two weeks later. His girlfriend didn't take him back though, she had already moved on.

Kretchmann was dead, killed by Gitta, not that Meg told them. Bliebtreu assumed his death was at Zachary's hands until Mailer put him straight the next day in his final report. It surprised him to hear that there had been a second werewolf, but it began to establish a pattern: Barnabus was looking for other shifters, first in Bremen and now here, and the Alliance had managed to identify several. Two were homeless who gladly joined the SIA when approached. Suddenly they had purpose but more than that they were being paid and had a roof over their heads for the first time in years. Bliebtreu wanted more; he wanted every supernatural he could recruit, but he wouldn't send vanilla humans after Barnabus again. Tomorrow, he would change the chase and dispatch the shifters.

Turning to Voss, he said, 'Call on the horn and call up Graf and Baer. Tell them to drop whatever case I have them on and get here. I am sending them after Barnabus.' Barnabus wouldn't be able to fight two of his own kind and maybe he would be more likely to listen to them.

Kiel didn't come out of his coma for six weeks, the injury to his skull didn't leave any lasting damage but Mailer's report of the incident was enough to convince Bliebtreu to fire him. They confiscated Gitta's body, telling the victim's mother they were arranging an autopsy, then they simply vanished with it. Back at the underground facility in Berlin, an autopsy revealed nothing. Bliebtreu wanted to know what was different about her. Something about her physiology allowed her to shift forms; if they understood it, maybe they could replicate it or work how to build a weapon that would stop it. But the team of doctors found nothing, one of them quipping, 'That's why it's called magic.'

Annoyed with his lack of progress, Bliebtreu closed the file on Barnabus and put it to one side. There was a new breakout of shilt attacks in Holland and he had been asked to send men to help; his were among the most experienced in Europe.

He sighed and picked up the phone, glancing again at his shifter file as he waited for the call to connect. He would find a way to recruit Barnabus. He had to. He was convinced that humanity's future depended on men like him. Something was coming, all the signs pointed to it. But like everyone else, he had no idea what that something might be.

Epilogue: Anastasia

Eight hundred kilometres away in Cheltenham, England, unaware of the supernatural, of the events unfolding at an old abandoned British army base, and completely oblivious to the part she would play in the planet's future, twenty-two-old Anastasia Aaronson was fighting with her mother.

'It doesn't matter what you say, mum. It's already done.'

'You're not going to Zannaria to fight in a war!' she raged.

Calmly, Anastasia sipped her tea, further infuriating her mother before she answered. 'You don't seem to have grasped the key point, mum. I am an officer in the British Army; I go where they send me, and I don't question my orders.'

'Well, you can ruddy well call them and tell them you can't go.' Her mother was going red in the face in her exasperation and anger.

'That is not an option,' Anastasia replied as she drained the last of her tea and placed the mug in the dishwasher. What bothered Anastasia most was that she first announced her intention to join the British Army when she was in her early teens. It was a show on television that caused the idea to form and take root. She distinctly remembered talking about it at the time but though her mother and sister both ignored her, assuming it was nothing more than a fanciful dream that would soon be replaced by the next, Anastasia's mind never wavered.

Her mother knew well in advance that her youngest daughter was going to join the army, but she refused to sign the paperwork, forcing Anastasia to wait for her eighteenth birthday to sign it for herself. Shamefully, when she graduated from Sandhurst Royal Military Academy, she was the only person on parade without her family proudly watching.

That was three years ago, and her mother was still waiting for Anastasia to admit it was all a huge mistake.

In the next room, Anastasia's older sister paused the television, not because she wanted to hear what they were shouting; she had heard it all before. The program was paused because she couldn't hear it over her mother's screeching.

Seeing an opportunity to poke fun, she shouted so her voice would carry to the kitchen. 'Why did you join the army anyway? Are you a lesbian?' She was being deliberately cruel, annoying her sister because Anastasia had a short fuse and it was fun to see how mad she got. 'Hey, I'm just saying that's what I heard about female soldiers,' she shouted, waiting to see if she could make Anastasia snap. 'All the girls in the army are gay. It's okay to be gay, Ana, you don't need to get upset about it, just come out of the closet and move on proudly.'

The two-word answer she got back didn't surprise her, but it threw more fuel on their mother's argument.

'I didn't raise you to use language like that,' she snapped.

'You barely raised me at all,' Anastasia fired back, knowing it was a cruel comment but relatively accurate, nevertheless. 'There are people out there who cannot fight for themselves mother. Someone needs to stand up to fight for them.'

'You're five feet tall,' her sister's voice rang out. 'They won't know even if you do stand up.'

Anastasia made a mental vow to get even with her sister later. She didn't bother to respond though, pointing out that she was, in fact, five feet and one inch would just encourage more abuse. There was no sense in speaking at all; her mother wouldn't listen and though her sister was a bully who badly needed to be taught a lesson, Anastasia wasn't going to be the one to teach it.

As she went up the stairs to her room, making a point to do so calmly and with dignified control, she heard her sister join her mother in the kitchen where she said, 'That one thinks she's going to save the world. All five feet of her.'

The End

Author Note:

H i there,

    I shall start by thanking you for reading my book. If you got this far and find yourself reading the author note, I will assume you enjoyed it and want some more.

It's late in my house as I write this little note at the end. The house is asleep, the only sounds to be heard are my fingers on the keyboard and my dachshund snoring beneath my bed as my wife sleeps. That's not a complaint on my part, I feel very lucky to be able to write stories that people buy and then love. I find myself in a flow with them, the words pouring from my head and onto the page via my fingers and that is why I was on my keyboard at 0500hrs this morning and find myself still there as it approaches midnight. Don't worry, I get up and move around sometimes.

I have a gym in the garden. Or more accurately, I have a log cabin in my garden that I use as my peaceful place for writing and in there I also have a gym. During my time in the army I never had to worry about getting saggy or soft or even concern myself with the danger of overindulging on calories. I used to put in ten hours or more physical exercise each week and then they would send me to Iraq or somewhere equally fun from where I was guaranteed to return looking like I had been vacuum-packed into my skin. Now though, I need to throw some weight around to stop myself from slowing becoming the Michelin Man.

Zachary Barnabus was a late addition to **The Realm of False Gods** series. I devised him while writing **Untethered Magic**, the first book from this series to be released even though it wasn't the first to be written. I needed someone to help the central character in *Untethered Magic* and to add a bit of colour and fun. He is immensely fun to write, as are all my characters, but there are some that stand out more than others, just due to their attitude, and Zachary is one of those.

He has several more books coming but if this is the first book in this series that you have read, then go back and pick up *Untethered Magic* and *Unleashed Magic* because Zachary is in both of those and they are a hoot.

I cannot yet determine how many books this series might run to, but it is likely to be a lot (I know, I know, a lot is not a standardised unit of measurement). I have at least five characters with their own series within the world who overlap and intertwine with each other and each of those will have multiple books before they reach the cataclysm that is to come. Anastasia, who you get the briefest introduction to in the epilogue, appears in *Damaged but Powerful* where you will begin to see the role she has to play in the end of the world.

Steve Higgs

Eccles, Kent

February 2020

More Books By Steve Higgs

Blue Moon Investigations
Paranormal Nonsense
The Phantom of Barker Mill
Amanda Harper Paranormal Detective
The Klowns of Kent
Dead Pirates of Cawsand
In the Doodoo With Voodoo
The Witches of East Malling
Crop Circles, Cows and Crazy Aliens
Whispers in the Rigging
Bloodlust Blonde – a short story
Paws of the Yeti
Under a Blue Moon – A Paranormal
Detective Origin Story
Night Work
Lord Hale's Monster
The Herne Bay Howlers
Undead Incorporated
The Ghoul of Christmas Past
The Sandman
Jailhouse Golem
Shadow in the Mine
Ghost Writer

Felicity Philips Investigates
To Love and to Perish
Tying the Noose
Aisle Kill Him
A Dress to Die For
Wedding Ceremony Woes

Patricia Fisher Cruise Mysteries
The Missing Sapphire of Zangrabar
The Kidnapped Bride
The Director's Cut
The Couple in Cabin 2124
Doctor Death
Murder on the Dancefloor
Mission for the Maharaja
A Sleuth and her Dachshund in Athens
The Maltese Parrot
No Place Like Home

Patricia Fisher Mystery Adventures
What Sam Knew
Solstice Goat
Recipe for Murder
A Banshee and a Bookshop
Diamonds, Dinner Jackets, and Death
Frozen Vengeance
Mug Shot
The Godmother
Murder is an Artform
Wonderful Weddings and Deadly
Divorces
Dangerous Creatures

Patricia Fisher: Ship's Detective Series
The Ship's Detective
Fitness Can Kill
Death by Pirates
First Dig Two Graves

Albert Smith Culinary Capers
Pork Pie Pandemonium
Bakewell Tart Bludgeoning
Stilton Slaughter
Bedfordshire Clanger Calamity
Death of a Yorkshire Pudding
Cumberland Sausage Shocker
Arbroath Smokie Slaying
Dundee Cake Dispatch
Lancashire Hotpot Peril
Blackpool Rock Bloodshed
Kent Coast Oyster Obliteration
Eton Mess Massacre
Cornish Pasty Conspiracy

Realm of False Gods
Untethered magic
Unleashed Magic
Early Shift
Damaged but Powerful
Demon Bound
Familiar Territory
The Armour of God
Live and Die by Magic
Terrible Secrets

About the Author

At school, the author was mostly disinterested in every subject except creative writing, for which, at age ten, he won his first award. However, calling it his first award suggests that there have been more, which there have not. Accolades may come but, in the meantime, he is having a ball writing mystery stories and crime thrillers and claims to have more than a hundred books forming an unruly queue in his head as they clamour to get out. He lives in the south-east corner of England with a duo of lazy sausage dogs. Surrounded by rolling hills, brooding castles, and vineyards, he doubts he will ever leave, the beer is just too good.

If you are a social media fan, you should copy the link below into your browser to join my very active Facebook group. You'll find a host of friends waiting there, some of whom have been with me from the very start.

My Facebook group get first notification when I publish anything new, plus cover reveals and free short stories, but more than that, they all interact with each other, sharing inside jokes, and answering question.

 facebook.com/stevehiggsauthor

You can also keep updated with my books via my website:

g https://stevehiggsbooks.com/

Printed in Great Britain
by Amazon

27829740R00098